EVERYTHING
BUT THE TRUTH

EVERYANTIMG
BUT
THE
TRUTH

Mandy Hubbard

SCHOLASTIC INC.

ISBN 978-1-338-03478-3

12 11 10 9 8 7 6 5 4 3 2 1   16 17 18 19 20 21

Printed in the U.S.A.   40

First Scholastic printing, January 2016

Book design by Amanda Bartlett
Typeset by Integra Software Services Pvt. Ltd.

For Bree Ogden—I hope you read this book, remember how amazing Seattle is, and move back. *Pitch Perfect* just isn't the same without you.

EVERYTHING BUT THE TRUTH

CHAPTER ONE

I found my new boyfriend, I type into my phone, and I'm about to walk into his apartment. ALONE!!

I click Send and dart a glance up and down the hall, but the building is silent. Not even the slightest muffled sounds resonate beyond the doors on either side of the corridor. Until my mom and I moved into the building three months ago, I didn't even know it was possible for a place to be filled with so many people and still be dead silent.

Especially since the shmancy-fancy decor looks like it should be accompanied by an orchestra or angels singing or something.

My phone chirps, and I open the reply from Alex, my best friend. How hot are his liver spots? Does he have any hair left?

I chuckle and shove my phone back into my pocket without replying, then pick up the tray from the polished, gleaming sideboard, careful not to knock over the towering vase of fresh flowers. Today it's peonies.

I step into apartment 204, bracing myself against what I know will happen next. I make it just three steps across the travertine tiles before I hear his gravelly voice, always a little off-key.

"*O Christmas tree, O Christmas tree,*" he belts out at the top of his lungs. The space is filled by his voice, followed by a deep, chest-rattling cough.

Even though the joke got old, oh, two months ago, and even though it's June twentieth, I can't keep from smiling at Mr. Graham, who very much has his own hair . . . even if it *is* Santa Claus white.

Actually, if the dude could grow a beard, he could probably work all December at Macy's.

Mr. Graham grins back, his eyes sparkling as if he's proud of his on-the-spot wittiness. But he knows he's been singing Christmas carols every time I walk into his apartment; unlike some of the other folks who live here, his memory is just fine.

"*How lovely are your branches,*" I sing back, in what is probably the second-worst singing voice in the world, after his. I'm really more of a classic art person than a *performing* arts person.

I set his lunch tray down on an oak barley-twist side table, careful not to knock over the glass of water I've brought. The table is almost a hundred years old, assuming it's not a reproduction.

I pull the stainless steel lid off his lunch with a dramatic flourish, like we're on a Food Network show and I just presented him with a gourmet lunch I crafted out of an absurd list of ingredients like wasabi peas and Pop-Tarts.

"Thanks, Holiday," he says, then drops the recliner's footrest with an ear-splitting screech. The man could probably have any chair he wants, but he sits in one that looks like it was purchased in 1982.

"Plain old Holly is fine," I say, removing the Saran Wrap from the top of his water glass. He doesn't need to know I'm not actually named after a holiday but instead the decidedly unglamorous Holiday Inn where my parents met.

"But then my Christmas carols won't make sense. And Holly is boring," he counters, "just like this chicken."

"Now, now, chicken is good for you," I say, resisting the urge to point out that it was cooked by an award-winning executive chef and his army of sous-chefs, so there's no way it's boring. "You know you're supposed to be watching your weight."

"I'm seventy-eight," he barks. "I don't give a crap about my weight."

I chuckle, pulling a Seattle Chocolates truffle from the pocket on my frilly lace apron. I don't have to wear it, but Sunrise House is kind of the best place in the world to wear an apron made entirely of patchworked doilies. Ms. Hannigan, in 208 down the hall, always gets a kick out of seeing me in something I made from a discarded box of her stuff. Plus I put a picture of it on Pinterest, and it has, like, nine hundred pins or something, proving that it's awesome. And if you ask me, I am rocking the *heck* out of this doily apron.

"I know." I drop the treat onto his plate. "But don't tell anyone I gave you that."

"Lips are zipped," he says, his eyes twinkling.

I try not to roll my eyes, because he's totally going to brag to his neighbor about having chocolate. One of these days I'm going to get into trouble for sneaking him so much sugar.

He unrolls his fabric napkin, spreading it out on his lap. "I ever tell you about the time I rode a horse into a bar?"

I grin. "About a thousand times, yes."

"*You* ride a horse into a bar and you can get lippy with me, missy."

"I'm not old enough to go into a bar," I say. "Even without the horse."

"Huh." He studies me, as if he just remembered I'm only eighteen.

Melodic chimes fill the air, and I glance at the antique grandfather clock in the corner of his apartment. "Whoops, gotta go," I say. "See you later!"

"Hold up," he says, waving his hand.

I try to hide my grin as I accept the tip he's holding out, bobbing my head. "Thanks."

He grunts in acknowledgment as I shove the five-dollar bill into my pocket. Another tip, another five bucks toward college.

He doesn't have to tip me. I'm not an official employee here. He could call the front desk and have someone else deliver it, since that's one of the many complimentary amenities available to residents.

But I bet the regular delivery people don't sneak him chocolate.

"Come back at dinner," he calls out.

I raise a finger and waggle it at him. "No way. Come to Amuse-Bouche tonight and *maybe* I'll hook you up with more sugar."

"I hate that silly restaurant. It's pompous and crowded."

I grin. Mr. Graham is one of the few residents who doesn't seem to enjoy his posh surroundings. Like his choice in chairs, he seems to prefer the more . . . *comfortable* things in life. I get the feeling his kids are the wealthy ones, not him—so he's endlessly out of place here.

Like me.

I can't say I blame him. Amuse-Bouche is the largest of Sunrise's three restaurants, but it *is* rather fancy, in an annoyingly self-aware kind of way. The name is French, I think, but I have no idea what it means.

"I know you hate it, but think of all the ladies who will miss you if you don't make an appearance . . . ," I say, purposely trailing off as I head to the door. He's still grumbling in his chair as I slip out of his apartment and back into the wide, bright halls of Sunrise House.

As the glossy brochure says, this place is where "we welcome your loved ones at the dawn of their most wonderful years!"

They leave out the part where they welcome only the ridiculously, preposterously rich. The place was built in a slightly open V shape, and almost the entire bottom floor, except for a few staff apartments, is reserved for the amenities. There are three restaurants, plus a spa, a ballroom where residents can take lessons with Blackpool champion ballroom dancers, an extra kitchen *just* for cooking lessons, and an opera-house-slash-theater for guest performances. We've had actual Broadway plays come through before they opened at the Fifth Avenue Theater in downtown Seattle.

The rooms, located on levels two through four, are large and luxurious, with marble floors and warm yellow paint. I think the color is supposed to remind people of gold. Like, I think they literally want people to remember how rich they are every time they look at the wall. And you can see Lake Washington from basically any apartment in this place.

Not long after I moved in here with my mom, I went on a walk, and I saw a tiny lot with lake frontage down the street. It was a million dollars for a postage-stamp-size plot of dirt. I mean, I knew Mercer Island was expensive. I guess people like that it's surrounded by Lake Washington, but it's not all cut off like a regular island, since it's connected to both Seattle and Bellevue by the I-90 bridges.

Sunrise House has some of the best lake frontage there is, wide and flat and green, with the most beautiful sunrise views I've ever seen, hence the name. So I don't even want to know how much the ten acres Sunrise House sits on is worth, let alone the building itself. But I guess they needed the expansive lot for the small marina, the tennis courts, and the wide green lawns with their sprawling pathways, said to be "perfect for that lazy Sunday afternoon stroll."

Plus, the leasing manager is the best money can buy.

And yeah, okay, the manager is my mom, but she *is* the best. She knows *exactly* how to bring in new residents, and she's already filled several vacant units in the three months since we moved in. I would know, because she celebrates every time, and I sip sparkling apple cider while she has champagne. And trust me, it tastes way better than the Capri Sun pouches I grew up on.

I round the bend in the hall—the turn that marks the center of the V—making my way back toward the front entry where Amuse-Bouche is located. According to the brochure, having on-site *restaurants* instead of dining halls or cafeterias makes the residents feel like they're on vacation and not put out to pasture. I mean, it didn't say it exactly like that, but I think that was the point they were making.

Ahead, forks and spoons clatter against what I know to be beautiful china. It looks like the special-occasion stuff people register for, for weddings or whatever, except they use it at every meal. I never even knew that was a thing until we moved in here. They're not even dishwasher safe, so some poor schmuck has to wash each plate by hand.

I pause near the enormous columns that circle the room like sentries guarding the residents. It's easy to see why they placed this restaurant so close to the front door—it embodies the whole Caesars Palace–esque, over-the-top luxury decor of Sunrise House, from soaring, coffered ceilings to the gilt-framed paintings to the Italian marble floors. They even make the waiters wear tuxedos.

Each table has crisp white tablecloths, and each place setting has two plates and, like, six pieces of silverware. This is why I've never eaten at Amuse-Bouche. I don't know how.

Three tables have family members present, but the others are the usual suspects—gray-haired ladies with glamorous designer dresses and long strings of pearls, and men in button-downs and blazers, looking like they're supposed to be smoking a pipe next to a crackling fireplace or something. I don't really get it. When I'm old, I'm totally rocking yoga pants and T-shirts.

I turn away, leaving the hustle and bustle of the restaurant behind as I head toward the soaring front entryway and my mom's office. On either side of me, the walls are adorned with enormous paintings in hand-carved antique frames. For a long time I thought the paintings were authentic . . . but there's no way the one near the front doors is an *actual* Donatello original, right?

Before we moved in, I always thought a place like this would be filled with still-life paintings. Like hotels are. Instead, I was pleasantly surprised at the utter lack of boring fruit bowls. I mean, I guess we *are* catering to millionaires who have better taste than my namesake, Holiday Inn, but still.

I continue past the restaurant, hitting the point where the ceiling soars to forty feet. I know the trim work is about ten years old, not centuries-old plaster, but every time I pass this spot, I can't help but look up. Can't help but admire the art, the craftsmanship, the utter awe that the view inspires. It's the closest to the Sistine Chapel I'll probably ever get.

I blink it away and get back to the real world. At my mom's office, I stop just outside the open door. Her space isn't quite as large as Mrs. Weaver's, the general manager, who is responsible for overseeing *everything* from housekeeping to nurses to entertainment for the residents. That lady has an office big enough for a gymnastics tumbling routine. She's also kind of intimidating, in a strict, no-nonsense librarian sort of way.

My mom's space may pale in comparison to Mrs. Weaver's, but it's impressive nonetheless, with windows that showcase the perfect view so prospective tenants can admire it while they sit in overstuffed leather chairs and sign their new leases. And besides—eight years and five moves ago, our entire apartment would've fit inside this office.

My mom is responsible for keeping the forty-two high-dollar units filled. The second floor has twenty of the super-popular one-bedroom units (which rent for a preposterous eight thousand dollars a month), the third floor has fourteen spacious apartments, and the fourth, the penthouse level, is home to eight sprawling suites, including the one known as the Waterview Suite, the best in the building because it sits at the center of the V and has a 180-degree view. I've jokingly started to call it the Watergate Suite because I heard someone say it was an "absolute scandal" that it hadn't been rented in over a year.

Despite the pressure, my mom's job is basically amazing. She has an *assistant*. Twelve years ago, she *was* the assistant. And while I always believed she'd make something of herself, her meteoric rise in the years since Dad bailed and left us to fend for ourselves is still a little shocking.

She's sitting behind a massive oak desk, her chin resting on one hand, her hair falling into her face. It's the same color as mine—a rich, deep brown shade, but hers is cut shorter, framing her chin.

"I'm done delivering lunches," I say as I step onto the Oriental rug that extends from the door to the front of her desk.

I found the rug in a back storage room the week after we moved in. It was an absolute tragedy that it had been rolled up and left to languish in a corner, so while my mom was giving someone a tour, I perfectly and artfully placed it in her office. Even *she* admits it works nicely—really pulls guests into her space, welcoming them in.

God, I'm lame.

"Okay. Thanks, Holly," she says, not bothering to glance up. Sometimes it's still weird to see her sit behind the massive desk and realize she belongs there. To realize it's *her* desk and she's not playing pretend, that all her hopes and dreams and promises actually came to fruition. She's got that framed diploma from the University of Washington—the one she worked so dang hard for—hanging on the wall, right beside my senior picture.

"I'll be in the billiards room if you need me," I say, waggling my eyebrows as I wait for her inevitable reaction. She's going to glance up and warn me not to rearrange the furniture, not to get any bright ideas.

I mean, all my ideas are bright. And we've been here three months now. Surely she's allowed to "optimize" the place a little to convince people they should move in. I so totally have her best interests at heart.

"Mm-hmm," she says instead.

I grin and turn to leave. "See ya later."

"Hold on a sec," she says.

I sigh internally. *So close.* I glance back. "Yeah?"

"Don't wait up for me for dinner. I have a bunch of stuff to get through. There's lunch meat in the fridge or Amuse-Bouche is serving beef Wellington. Caliente is closing down for a private party at eight."

"Okay," I say, even though I don't know what beef Wellington is. "See you . . . whenever."

And then I beat a hasty exit.

Billiards room, here I come.

CHAPTER TWO

An hour later, I'm huffing and puffing as I lean in, my hands gripping the carved wooden armrest as I shove, hard, on the couch. It moves only an inch.

An inch.

Stupid freakin' behemoth couch. I feel like I'm trying to move a Mack truck. Trees must have weighed more in the seventeenth century.

Yeah, that makes sense.

I groan and push again, straining with all my might. The leg screeches against the marble floor and then gives way, sliding abruptly. My hands slip off the armrest, and I slam to the ground.

"Oomph," I say, my forehead resting on the cool floor that had, moments ago, been covered by a French provincial sofa.

The ground is musty. Dusty. Like, oh, I don't know, it's been covered by a couch for a few decades. I've gotten so used to the polished-until-I-can-see-my-reflection cleanliness in this place that it's almost foreign to smell actual dirt.

Footsteps shuffle closer, and I suddenly realize I'm not alone. Crap, I hope my mom isn't going to bust me. . . .

I roll over and look up into the amused, warm brown eyes of a boy close to my age. He's leaning over, resting his hands on his knees as he peers down. I blink as if he's a mirage and he'll disappear. Spotting a guy like him in a place like this is harder than finding a lifeboat on the *Titanic*.

But he doesn't.

Disappear, that is.

Awesome. The first boy under seventy I've seen in this place, and he finds me lying facedown on the floor of the billiards room.

"It was the candlestick," I say abruptly, because it's the only thing I can think of and I'm fighting the urge to check him out.

He's cute. Really, really cute. He looks . . . Costa Rican. Maybe part Native American or part African American . . . or some combination uniquely his, because I've never seen a guy so totally drool worthy.

In a place like this, a place filled with rich, elderly white people, he stands out, dazzling in a way that has nothing to do with race, and everything to do with . . .

I blink, realizing that while I've been staring, his lips have been moving.

". . . was the sofa?" he asks, furrowing his brow as he walks around so that he can face me as I sit up.

"Oh, uh, no, the sofa's a little too heavy to use as a weapon. It was definitely the candlestick," I say, and then jut my thumb in the direction of an antique brass candelabrum. "And Professor Plum. Because he's weird-looking and I don't trust him."

One side of his mouth curls up as he reaches out to me.

I study him for a second before finally reaching out to accept his hand. It's warm and soft and strong, and he easily pulls me to my feet. And then I'm standing close to him. So close, I can smell him.

Cinnamon. I breathe deeper, enjoying the warm spiciness of it. Yes, he smells like cinnamon. As I rake in another breath, I catch him staring.

Abruptly I step away, realizing I'm standing within inches of him, just breathing him in over and over like an idiot.

"Ahhh," he says, once he has room to talk without speaking directly into my ear. "Because we're in the billiards room, of course."

"Yeah," I say, suddenly realizing how lame and outdated my joke is. Maybe if I didn't play board games with old people all the time . . .

To avoid looking at him, I dust off the seat of my pants and focus *really hard* on my apron.

Oh god. I'm wearing a doily apron in front of a hot boy. "I always pegged it on Mrs. Peacock," he says.

"Oh?" I ask, wondering if there's a way to ditch the apron without looking like it's because of him. I glance around, but it's not like there's a phone booth where I can go from the bumbling Clark Kent to the ultra-suave Superman. I don't even have a pair of glasses to take off. "Why's that?"

"She's the only one not named after a color."

I furrow my brow. "That's not true. Peacock is a color."

"Are you sure?" he asks, crossing his arms. I'm now very well aware of how built this boy is. He has serious muscles. Glorious, beautiful muscles, evident even through his stark white button-down and perfectly tailored black vest. He looks like he just left a wedding reception and lost his jacket somewhere.

"Yeah, it's a shade of blue. All the characters in Clue are colors," I say, realizing in some corner of my mind that's still functioning that I should probably shut up about Clue.

"I'll have to take your word for it," he says, flashing a cocky grin. He reaches out toward my face, and I freeze, half-expecting him to caress my cheek like something from a romance novel. But he doesn't. Instead, he touches my hair, then pulls his hand away.

The way he looks at me, amusement glimmering in his eyes as he turns his hand and reveals a dust bunny, it's like he *knew* what he was doing. Like he knew I'd think he was reaching out for . . . some other reason. And I fell for it.

Sheesh, I am so totally deprived of flirting-with-a-cute-guy opportunities, living in a retirement home with my mom. I need to get out more. I need to get a hobby or something before I swoon at his feet and ask if he wants to play bridge.

He smirks. "Sorry, it was kind of clinging to your ponytail. It was distracting."

"Well, I find your hair distracting too," I say, and then immediately wish I had just kept my trap shut.

I find your hair distracting? That was the best I could do?

"Really," he says, his eyebrow quirking. I realize then that his eyebrows are better groomed than mine. One of them, the right one, has two slashes through it, like he had it trimmed that way. Like he had them . . . sculpted to match the lines where his hair is buzzed shorter and little lines swoop and twirl on the sides of his head.

And I'm wearing an apron made of doilies.

"Yeah," I say, my face warming. "Your haircut is, um, crooked."

He smiles, that same amusement as earlier glittering in his eyes. "It's *supposed* to be crooked."

My laughter sounds like a barking seal having a seizure, and I can't believe he doesn't back away. Instead, his eyes light up, like my reaction surprises him.

"So you walked into the salon and said, 'Hi, I'd like a crooked haircut?'" I cross my arms, realize I look confrontational, and drop them again. Why do my arms feel so big all of a sudden? It's like I forgot how to function. Like my limbs have become giant noodles attached to my body and I have no control of them.

He laughs, a surprisingly deep, smooth-as-honey laugh that makes my stomach do a flip. "I go to a barber," he says, twisting his big silver watch in circles on his wrist. "And I let him do whatever he wants."

"Brave," I say, motioning with my hands in ridiculous wavy and jerky movements and *oh god what am I doing?*

"He's been cutting my hair for eighteen years," he replies, following my movement with his eyes, his lips twitching.

Oh great, he's picked up the fact that I live in Awkward City, USA. I've become entertainment.

And then his reply finally registers. Eighteen years. So he is at least eighteen years old. Probably nineteen. Although who knows, guys like him probably were born with sculpted hair and Armani suits, so he could still be just eighteen.

I swallow, breathing deeply and trying to calm my racing heart. "And did you like it?"

"Like what?"

"The crooked haircut," I reply, twisting my fingers into the edges of my lace apron. Are my palms damp? Were they damp when he pulled me to my feet or is this a new development? What if I have the dampest palms in the entire world and he's just really good at hiding his disgust?

"I did until now," he says, one side of his lips curling up as he meets my gaze, like an open challenge.

"Oh," I say, embarrassment creeping in. "I mean, it's a good haircut. It, uh, looks good on you."

"Right," he says. "Clearly, you adore it."

I blush harder now, my face so hot I'm sure he could feel it if he reached out and touched it. If he let his beautiful, long fingers slide across my cheek . . .

I clear my throat. "Um, I mean it. Crookedness and all."

"Mm-hmm," he says, still peering into my eyes as he smirks.

I'm suddenly, completely sure that no one has ever insulted his hair before. Or his looks. Or . . . him at all. So I basically freeze, staring right back at him, thinking that I've ruined any chance I had with him.

"I was voted best hair, you know," he says after I don't speak.

"I can see why," I say, then wish I hadn't. I want to know who voted him best hair. Other than me.

He laughs, and it feels the tiniest bit like it's at me, before he turns away for the first time and studies the couch. With his side to me, I can see the way his button-down strains across his shoulders, the full bulk of his arms under the shiny fabric. Silk. Is it silk? I'm not as good at fashion as I am at art and furniture. Not *high* fashion, anyway. My expertise is limited to cotton and doilies.

"What are you trying to do with this?"

"Move it over there," I say, pointing across the room, relieved to finally have something else to talk about.

"Why?"

"Because every time I walk by this room, it bugs me that it's set up entirely wrong. So I'm fixing it."

"But if you stick it in the middle of the room, won't it kind of . . . I don't know, block things off? I mean, this is one *giant* couch."

"No," I say. "Look at this thing. It's pretty much a piece of art. If I position it correctly, it will provide flow, *and* people will actually notice it and appreciate the design. And over here," I say, pointing to where I'd face-planted, "it blocks the window."

"Provides flow, huh?"

I might have been self-conscious about my Clue references, but my interior-decorating skills—no matter how dorky they are—never actually embarrass me. If you ask Alex, she'll say it's totally mortifying, but whatever.

"There's an actual science to interior decorating. Just like there's a science to how restaurants lay out their menu to highlight the big-ticket items, and grocery stores position impulse buys."

"I don't think I've ever met a teenage interior-decorating scientist," he says, crossing his arms. "And I know some pretty impressive people."

"Yeah? Like who?"

He shrugs. "Pop stars. Actresses. Inventors. The president's daughter."

"Try not to brag or anything," I say, rolling my eyes to pretend I'm unimpressed.

But really . . . who the heck is this boy? How does he know these people? And why would he bother talking to me when obviously he could go hang out with way cooler people? People who have full function of their arms, for instance.

"Hey, you asked," he says, one side of his mouth quirking up.

Okay, the boy is smokin' hot and knows it. The part of me all wound up at his attractiveness unravels. I will not be intimidated by insanely good looks and a crappy personality.

I meet his eyes, annoyed. "So, fine, you know impressive people, and I'm not one of them. Maybe you think this is stupid, but it's kind of my thing. So if you're not going to help me, maybe you should just move on?"

"Huh," he says, but not like I've irritated him. More like . . . he's intrigued. Like maybe I won him over. "Malik." He extends his hand. "And you are?"

"Lucy," a voice calls out just as I'm reaching for his hand. I swing around to find one of the residents, Henrietta, standing at the entryway, leaning against the doorjamb for support. My stomach sinks. Interlude with the Hot Boy is officially over. Henrietta is seventy-four and frail, and if she needs my help, it's more important.

"Sweetie, can you help me to my room?"

"Sure," I say, pretending like it's totally no big deal that I'm going to spend the entire summer dateless and pathetic. I step away from Malik as he drops his hand back to his side. "See you around?" I give him an awkward little wave. *Dumb.* I should have shaken his hand instead, if only to feel his skin, hot against mine, one more time. Maybe that would be enough cute-boy contact to last me the two months until I head off to college.

I make it all the way to the door before he answers.

"Yeah, see you later, Lucy."

I open my mouth to correct him just as Henrietta finds the crook of my elbow and leans against me. She always thinks I'm her granddaughter, Lucy, who was around my age when she died in a car wreck.

Once, I corrected her. Once, I told her the truth. But watching her eyes fill with tears as if hearing the news for the first time ensured I'll never do that again.

And I don't have the heart to do so now. To tell her my name isn't Lucy, that she has no family left at all, just a giant bank account and no one to leave it to.

And so I simply glance back at Malik one more time, searing his image in my head as I lead Henrietta back to her apartment.

By the time I return to the billiards room twenty minutes later, he's gone.

But the couch is sitting in the middle of the room, exactly where I wanted it.

CHAPTER THREE

"I'm thinking of doing my hair like this tomorrow," I say, pointing to the screen of my new MacBook. It was a graduation-slash-going-off-to-college present from my mom. My first laptop ever. It's shiny and perfect and beautiful. And, at the moment, it's open to my hairstyle album on Pinterest.

Alex leans closer to the screen, studying the intricate twisted pattern. "It's cute."

"Can I try it on you first?" I ask.

"Sure."

I don't have to explain to her what I want. We've played this game for years. Alex cares as much about hair and makeup and clothes as I do about her beloved Seattle Sounders, the local major league soccer team. I mean, just sitting through Alex's varsity soccer games was enough sports to last me an entire lifetime.

She's always been willing to play guinea pig, though, to all my crazy hair and makeup ideas. She's never made fun of my attempts to sew my own clothes, either.

I get up from my rolling computer chair, and she plunks right in and drops it as low as it goes. She immediately clicks over to iTunes and starts up the playlist she created months ago from my music library. It's not until the first song comes on that I realize how long it's been since we've done this. I chew on my lip, trying to remember when she was over last.

Before graduation. Two . . . no, three weeks ago. That was the last time.

We used to get together every day. I know this isn't the coolest place to hang out, in a two-bedroom apartment at a retirement home, but it's the best place I've ever lived, and the first time I've ever actually *liked* having friends over. Our apartment isn't far off from the entryway and the restaurants, since my mom needs to be able to meet potential residents at any time, but it's quiet in here. Really, it could be any apartment in any building in the world.

Except this one is mine, and it's way better than anything that came before it.

I part her hair straight down the middle, then twist one half up and clip it out of my way.

"So I met this guy yesterday," I say as my fingers tangle in her hair.

"The liver-spotted boyfriend?"

I grin. "No, he was, like, eighteen or nineteen or something."

"Where the heck did you meet a guy our age *here*?"

"Down the hall," I say. "The billiards room near the eleva-tors. I don't know why he was here. Maybe he visits old folks' homes for fun."

"Because he loves Werther's Originals," she says, tipping her head back as she laughs.

I grin. "Sit still. I'm trying to do the twisty thing."

"Sorry. I just like to picture you finding the one guy who would fit in here with you."

I chew on my lip and try to ignore the unintentional barb. It's stupid but . . . Alex doesn't really *like* this place. Not the way I do. Being here is like a really cool blend of art history and *Antiques Roadshow* and, I don't know, awesome stories and really nice people.

It's a new feeling for me, liking where I live. The places I've lived before were . . . um, a little rough. Not the last one, but the one before that, and definitely the one before that.

Alex has lived on the same quiet street, in a big, meticu-lously restored Craftsman house just a few blocks from Lake Washington, for as long as I've known her. We met at school back when my dad still cared about me and my mom enough to send child support, so we could afford to live in one side of an old but decently maintained duplex in the heart of Mercer Island. No view, but good schools and a quiet neighborhood.

Once he dropped off the face of the earth, we had to move off the island so my mom could make rent by herself.

For the first few years after my dad split, I lived in South Seattle, which is, like, not even in the same stratosphere as this neighborhood. But that was where we had to go for my mom to get her first job as a property manager—to a run-down, rat-infested apartment complex. And then a year later, we moved to a slightly less run-down, not-quite-infested elderly apartment complex. And then to a modest middle-class retirement complex. There was a big chunk of time where Alex and I didn't go to the same school, and our friendship survived on parks and playdates.

And then, eventually, we got here. To the lap of luxury. A nonstop ladder climb, fueled by my mom's pretty much living off caffeine and dreams.

Alex has never had to transfer schools like me, or put out rat bait. She doesn't realize what a place like this means.

"Anyway, was he cute?"

I blink away the flash of annoyance, and focus, again, on her hair. "Beyond cute. Tall, with the most amazing smile. His name's Malik."

"Everyone is tall compared to you."

I tug on her hair because she's always teasing me about my height.

"Yeah, yeah, sorry. So anyway, what happened?"

"Nothing. We talked for a few minutes, but I had to run off and help a resident. I probably won't see him again."

"Bummer."

I slip a bobby pin into her hair near the base of her neck, securing the twisty-twirly thing I've been arranging on the right side of her head. Alex's hair always goes into fancy updos so easily. It's pure irony that the sporty girl who wears nothing but ponytails would actually be a hairdresser's dream. I pull the clip off the left side, letting her hair fall back around her shoulders.

"Plus, he thinks my name is Lucy."

She laughs under her breath. "Why?"

"You know how I told you there's a lady on the fourth floor who thinks I'm her granddaughter? She showed up and called me that. She always does. She's the one I had to help." I frown. "He's out of my league, anyway. He dresses like he bought all his clothes in Paris or something."

"Hot."

"I know, he was, but I think—"

The door behind us swings open and bounces off the wall. I glance back, across the great room of our apartment. We've never had a great room before. I only know that's what it's called because my mom has all these floor plans she gives to prospective residents.

Between my mom and me is a big, overstuffed floral couch—the beautiful furniture this apartment came with is another perk of the job. It's not antique, like some of the pieces in the common areas, but it's still pretty nice stuff.

My mom staggers through the door with an armful of files in one hand and a giant vase of flowers in the other. I drop Alex's hair and cross the room, grabbing the files out of her arm before she drops them.

"What's this stuff?"

"The paperwork is on our new resident. And the flowers are the welcome bouquet I sent to his room, and which he's apparently allergic to."

"Oh." I glance over my mom. Her hair is sticking up at odd angles, her makeup is looking a little melty, and she's pretty much perspiring through her shirt. "Uh, something wrong?"

She sighs, blowing her bangs off her forehead. "It's only his second day here, but I can tell he's not impressed. I should have known about the flowers."

"I'm sure it's not a big deal," I say. "They're pretty. It's the thought that counts, right?"

"I'm not so sure thoughts matter very much to Charles Buchannan."

My jaw drops, and Alex whistles.

"*The* Charles Buchannan?" she asks.

My mom nods, her smile grim. "He just moved into the vacant penthouse suite."

I raise a brow. My mom's been talking nonstop about finding someone to rent the Watergate Suite since we moved in here. One month's rent could probably buy me a very nice car, which is why my mom has been sure that filling the unit would impress Mrs. Weaver, and, in turn, impress the bigwigs who swing by periodically for inspections. I'm not totally clear on how it works, but I think they're the ones who matter—they own what my mom calls a portfolio of retirement homes, and if she can get on their good side, she's golden.

"Why would a guy like him move here? If he needs assistance, he could hire two dozen personal assistants and chefs and nurses and stuff and just stay at home."

"His daughter set it up," she says, straightening the files. "She's worried about him becoming too withdrawn. She said he was halfway to becoming the next Howard Hughes, and she hopes an environment like Sunrise House will force him to socialize. Maybe take part in some of our scheduled excursions—you know, get out and about. I kind of promised if she could get him here that I'd take care of the rest. All I could get out of her was a ninety-day lease, so I've gotta figure out something soon."

"Oh," I say, racking my brains for everything I know about Charles Buchannan, but all I come up with is: dark-skinned; gray-haired; a mole on his right cheek; and obscenely, filthy rich. His place is across the bridge from here, to the east—toward Bellevue. He owns the largest estate on Lake Washington, after Bill Gates. I read an article once that said he bought three of his neighbors' houses and bulldozed them so he'd have more room for his gardens.

His company is growing so fast, some people think it could overtake Amazon as the biggest online retailer. Except there's one key difference: Buchannan sells only American-made products. Even the paper they use for shipping slips is from timber harvested by American timber companies. The man has made a bajillion dollars *and* he smells like roses, because he's single-handedly revived a bunch of different companies and even whole towns, like Aberdeen, a town on the Pacific Ocean a couple of hours away. It was slowly turning into a ghost town, once their lumber mill went out of business. Charles Buchannan selected Aberdeen to supply the pulp for his shipping boxes, and now their economy is booming again.

"Apparently, ever since he retired as CEO of Buchannan Industries two years ago, he's been a real hermit. She said he hasn't left his house in six months. I made all those promises thinking she'd never get him here. It sounded like a pipe dream."

"But he actually agreed to her plan?" I ask. "To move in, I mean."

She shrugs. "He's here, isn't he? But likely not for long if I don't go over all these files again. I should have known about his allergies. Two minutes on Google and I found it."

"You shouldn't have to Google your residents," I say. There are other people who handle the residents' day-to-day needs. "Your job is just to get them here, right? You were welcoming him, being friendly. It was a nice gesture."

"He's not just any resident. He expects the best. And I convinced his daughter this place was the answer to her worries. If he leaves because of me . . ." Her voice trails off and she sighs deeply, rubbing her eyes. "Plus, he knows I convinced her to send him here. He pretty much hates me."

It's been a while since I've seen her this worried. Watching her stand in the middle of the room but be mentally somewhere else slams me back into all the places we've been, all the jobs she's had, all the sacrifices she made to get here.

My mom has less than three months left of her six-month probationary period for this job, and then she can finally relax. I'll be able to go to Washington State University, like I always wanted to, and she'll be able to help me with my tuition.

If she loses this job, it'll kill her, and I can kiss WSU goodbye. It'll be community college and student loans.

We *both* need her to keep this job.

"They're really pretty, though," I say, reaching out and running my thumb over a silky petal. "If he weren't allergic, he would have loved them, I bet." I pick up the vase again and sniff. It's a gorgeous bouquet of white and blue hydrangeas, the perfect choice for a guy's room.

"Can I have them for my desk?" I ask.

"Sure, take them. I'm going to freshen up and then study this paperwork," she says, and disappears into her room. I hear her start up the shower in her master bathroom.

I turn to head to my room, and I'm halfway there when I glance over at Alex, who is busy typing something into Google. Just as I'm about to pass the screen, a matrix of images comes up.

I'm so startled that I nearly drop the flowers and have to dive to catch them before they hit the hardwood. Water from the vase splashes over my arms, but I hardly take my eyes off the monitor as Alex clicks one of the images and it expands, filling the screen.

It's *Malik*, in a suit and tie. It's some kind of red carpet event or something, because there's a black-and-white background with the words *American Music Awards* splashed across it. Malik's standing there, his broad shoulders perfectly squared, with that same smirk I saw earlier—the one that says he owns the world and he knows it.

"What—how did you do that?" I ask, climbing back to my feet and setting the vase on the desk next to the computer.

"When your mom said *Buchannan*, something clicked." Alex turns to me, her hair half up and half down, a smug grin on her face. "Malik Buchannan. Grandson of the third richest man in America."

I turn back to the screen. I blink again and again, waiting for the image to change, but it doesn't.

It's him.

"You're right about one thing," she says, her finger tracing along the lapel of his crisp black suit jacket.

"What?" I ask, ripping my gaze from the screen to look at her again.

"He probably shops in Paris."

An hour later I'm sitting on my bed, listening to the *click-click-click* of the keys on my laptop as Alex pulls up another article on the *New Yorker*'s Web site. The sound echoes through my room. I know my space isn't as big as most of the rental units upstairs, but it's the first time in a few years that I haven't needed to share a room with my mom.

My room is clean, large, and bright. It came with the queen-size bed I am currently sprawled across, including the antique-white, four-poster frame. There's a matching dresser and a desk I used to study for finals. Above us, the ceilings are twelve feet tall, with recessed lights that highlight the deep-pile, crème-colored carpet on the floor. A month after we moved in, my mom even replaced my ratty, twin-size comforter with a thick, poufy purple one.

Seriously, it's perfect.

"I don't know if I believe this one about Selena Gomez. They were probably just at the same event or something. Wasn't she with Justin Bieber back then?"

"Does it matter? Selena, Vanessa, Emma Watson . . . He dates the Who's Who of Hollywood. I mean, god, he did say he knows impressive people. I just didn't realize he meant *that* impressive."

"So?"

"So . . ." I say, drawing out the words. How can she not see the problem here? "I don't stand a chance. I sew my own clothes and I geek out over furniture."

She twists around in her chair. "But he sounds like he was into you. I mean, I thought you said he was flirting."

"I don't know. It was kind of hard to tell if he was flirting or making fun of me. You know, like 'hahaha, let's play with the peasant girl.' I mean, I didn't tell him I was poor, but it's not like he couldn't see my clothes and figure it out. And god, you should've seen me. I looked like a newborn robot. Herky-jerky and awkward."

She rubs her lips together for a moment, as if considering the idea. "Before you knew he was disgustingly rich, did it seem like flirting?"

I try to remember everything he said to me, every smile and glance. "Yeah. But maybe kind of like he would flirt with anyone. Like it's a sport."

"Okay. So then we need to get you in front of him again. Preferably with me there."

"Why?"

"Because he's hot and wealthy and you totally need to marry him someday, but you are, like, *really* bad at this," she says, laughter in her voice. "So I'm going to help you."

Without looking, I grab the pillow off my bed and hurl it at her.

"Hey! I was kidding. Sort of. Okay, maybe not really. I mean, you suck at flirting with boys. Even I know that."

"I do not."

"You have dated precisely one boy, Hunter, and he was really adorable but dumb as rocks. This guy is hot and rich and basically everything you could want in your life. Yeah, you'll need backup."

"You're being shallow."

"And you're being dishonest with yourself. You know you want him. I mean, look at this guy. He's the whole package. Besides, if *you're* not going to make it happen . . ."

"Oh, whatever."

"Just think of the secluded, private mansion he probably lives in. You could check out his . . ." Her voice trails off and she wiggles her eyebrows. ". . . Antiques."

I laugh. "I am neither marrying him nor admiring his *antiques*."

"Fine," she says, closing out the Web browser. "Then what do you want to do with our day?"

"What time is it?"

"Four."

"Already? I was going to work for a couple more hours."

"Ugh, really?" she asks, her lip curling up.

"I know it's not technically a paid gig, but they always tip me for the personalized service. That stuff adds up. I made forty bucks just yesterday. I mean, how *else* am I going to pay for college?"

Alex plays with the tendril of hair I left out of her fancy updo. "Why do you do that?"

I sit up. "Do what?"

She laughs. "Spend all your free time with some old people you're not even related to. There are better ways to earn a buck."

"First of all, they like me. Henrietta even bought me a birth-day present. I mean, it wasn't actually my birthday; it was Lucy's," I say, making air quotes. "But still. It was sweet."

"She thinks you're someone you're not."

"You know I can't change that." I roll off my bed, climbing to my feet. "And I'm not *hanging out* with them anyway. All I do is bring them a few meals or grab their mail or walk their dogs, and they tip me like crazy. And they know there are actual employees for this stuff, but the staff doesn't mind. The residents like that I take my time to get to know them and make a little bit of small talk. I know it's ridiculous. But I don't even care because I like getting to know them too. Besides, I have, like, seven hundred dollars saved already, and I only started doing this last month."

"Oh, well," she says. "If you weren't busy, I was going to invite you to EMP with me and Rena. They have a new exhibit on Britney Spears."

Something painful hits me square in the chest. The Experience Music Project. A crazy, wonky-shaped building next to the Space Needle. We've talked about going to EMP off and on forever. I mean, Rena is our friend too—well, mostly Alex's from school—but we were supposed to plan our visit together. Instead of pointing that out, though, I simply say, "Okay, have fun. Text me some pictures or something. Supposedly they have the hair she shaved off when she went crazy."

She fist-bumps me on her way out the door, and then I'm alone again. I drag myself off my bed and go to the kitchen and grab a handful of Skittles from the funky crystal bowl on the counter. Another perk of the apartment. I'm afraid to ask where it came from, how much it cost. It'll probably turn out to be some ridiculous designer bowl worth two hundred dollars or something, and here I poured Skittles into it.

I chew them slowly, staring out across our apartment. I still remember the moment we walked in, after my mom found out she had the job and she got the keys, and I took in the floral couch; the built-in maple bookcases; the brand-new, sparkling-clean carpets; the granite-topped kitchen table with four shiny new chairs, all with matching floral seat cushions.

It's the most *full* apartment I've ever lived in, without a scrap of shabby, broken-down furniture. We're not going to lose it. Not if I can help it.

I grab another handful of Skittles, then drag my butt out of our apartment.

I head to the front desk first, where a twentysomething blonde sits, leaned over a notebook, the phone pressed to her ear. She glances up and smiles at me, mouthing, *One minute.*

I lean on the counter, waiting as she finishes scribbling something down.

"Hey, Julia," I say when she hangs up the phone. "Any requests today?"

"Um, yeah," she says, flipping back a couple of pages in the notebook. She knows I'm not an *actual* employee, but she still takes notes for me. Probably because anything I do is one less thing for the paid staff. I mean, I'm sure she knows I accept tips, but since I'm not an employee, there's no rule against it. The employees can't take the cash. It's part of the handbook or something.

"Four-oh-five called almost an hour ago. She was hoping you'd take her dog out."

Henrietta. She's got a little bichon frise with fluffy white fur. I kind of adore the silly thing.

"Cool," I say. "Thanks." I leave the front lobby behind and head to the elevator, punching the number four, the level for the penthouse suites.

When the elevator arrives, I step off into the hall, rounding the bend.

I find Henrietta kneeling half out of her open door in front of an overturned pot, a handful of soil in her hands.

"What happened?" I ask, rushing over and dropping to my knees beside her. She barely gets around with her walker—she should *not* be kneeling in the hall.

"I was going to go down and watch a movie in the theater, and I tripped," she says. "On my welcome mat."

"Are you okay? Does anything hurt?"

"I'm fine, I think," she says.

"Let's get you up. You can sit on the bench and I'll fix the plant." I gently pull her to her feet. "Are you sure you're okay?"

I lean down, dusting a few pieces of soil off her beautiful rose-colored slacks. Luckily, they look like they survived the encounter okay. They probably cost more than my entire wardrobe.

"I think so. Just a short tumble," she says, laughing at her own joke.

I grin. Henrietta is less than five feet tall, and she's got a great sense of humor about it. It's kind of taught me to embrace my own five-foot-one status with a little more grace. "Well, it looks like your clothes are okay too. Let me just—"

"Lucy," a voice calls out.

I spin around to see Malik striding down the hall, and I instantly wonder how I ever thought he was a mere mortal like me. He's wearing a tailored blazer that hugs his frame and a button-down shirt left open at the collar, over the most glorious blue jeans I've ever seen. He belongs on a billboard for Swiss watches or men's cologne or something.

"Malik," I say, and instantly, my cheeks burn fire-hot. Ugh, this guy is so heart-stoppingly gorgeous I can't even say one word without blushing.

"I wondered if I'd see you again," he says, the words slipping out easily, like I could be one of a hundred girls he probably hopes to see on a daily basis.

He stops in front of me and flashes that red-carpet smile I'd seen on my computer. The one he used when he looked at Selena Gomez or Emma Watson.

"Yeah, I mean, I'm here all the time." I dart a look at Henrietta, who is watching the exchange with bright eyes.

"My Lucy visits me every day," she says.

"Uh, yeah," I say, turning away from Malik and swallowing the words I need to say.

I need to tell him who I am—not Lucy, but Holly, just some nobody who lives in a retirement home. But I can't do it in front of Henrietta, unless I want her to burst into tears.

I drop back to my knees and try to adjust the poor little fern that got dumped onto the floor. It's totally askew and has lost half of its dirt. I pick up the first handful of soil, and then Malik is beside me, grabbing fistfuls of dirt and dropping them into the pot, and I feel the sudden urge to fill the silence.

"It's a good thing I got here," I whisper, just low enough so that Henrietta won't hear.

"Why?"

"Because pot kills," I joke.

Malik snorts, and it turns into an awkward, adorable chuckle.

When I drop another handful into the pot, our hands brush, and it's like a bolt of electricity.

And I know he feels it because he looks up to meet my eyes just as I search for his, and for almost a breath we remain absolutely still. I swear if Henrietta weren't staring at us, he'd kiss me. Instead, I'm the first to turn away.

"I think that's the most we can get with our hands." I climb to my feet. "I'll go find a vacuum."

"Don't they have staff for that?" he asks, standing beside me.

"Uh, what?" I ask.

"Staff. Maids or whatever. Just call them," he says, waving his hand in the air, like it's the easiest, most obvious choice, something he's used to doing. Just . . . calling people to take care of things.

I'm suddenly, acutely aware of our differences in class and in upbringing. He assumes my family has the tens of thousands of dollars *per month* needed to stay at a place like this. Just like his grandfather.

And so he assumes I'll just . . . *call the staff.*

When I practically am one.

"Oh, uh, yeah. Henrietta? Do you still want to go to the movie? I can help you downstairs . . ."

She waves her hand. "I've had enough excitement now. And I just remembered that *The Price Is Right* started," she says, frowning. "I missed the first half."

"I set it to record for you, remember? I'll get it going. You haven't missed a thing, promise."

Malik pushes the half-open door all the way in, and we lead her inside. My shoes clack on the marble entry, echoing off the fourteen-foot ceilings. We pass the little parlor off the entry, stepping into the wide-open living room. I know I'm not technically related to Henrietta, but her exquisite taste in furniture makes me feel like I could be. She likes stuff from the Victorian period. Her sofa is rosewood and leather, with intricately carved armrests and bolster cushions. I will literally drool if I stare at it too long.

I deposit her on one end of the couch, then click on her program and give her a brief hug. Then I'm back out in the hall, standing next to Malik, acutely aware of the fact that I'm standing next to one of the hottest, richest guys in the country.

"Uh, thanks for your help," I say.

"No problem. She seems sweet," he says.

"Um, yeah, she's awesome."

I should tell him that I have to go get a vacuum to clean up the carpet and that Henrietta is not my relative and that he's way too out of my league to be looking at me with that smile.

Also, I definitely should not smile back.

Too late.

"Come with me to visit with my grandpa," he says. "I think he's sick of me and he'd probably rather look at a pretty girl anyway."

Pretty? He thinks I'm pretty? I forget everything I wanted to tell him.

"Unless you're busy," he says after I don't reply.

"Oh. Uh, no. I mean, if you're sure it's okay . . ."

"Of course," he says, reaching for my hand. "Come on."

Oh god, oh god, oh god, I'm holding hands with Malik Buchannan. The same hand that has held Emma Watson's. I try my best to act casual, like the way he's tugging on my fingers is just . . . a friendly thing, meaningless. As if I've had a million smart, older, sophisticated boyfriends like him.

I think my hands are getting damp again though. Maybe this is a real problem and they make over-the-counter, anti-palm dampness pills I should look into.

I really *should* come clean, but the urge to meet Charles Buchannan, a name synonymous with Bill Gates and Steve Jobs and Richard Branson, is overwhelming . . . almost as heady as the feel of Malik's fingers intertwined with my own.

Henrietta's room is at one end of the hall, but Charles's place is at the center of the V, and there aren't any doors nearby. I guess that's because of the size of his unit, the way it sprawls in both directions.

Malik pulls me down the hall, and we pause at the door. It looks like all the others on this floor—dark-stained wood with six recessed panels—except that it has a different knocker.

"Wait, is that new?" I ask, narrowing my eyes and trying to make out the shapes and contours of the brass.

"Yeah. It's our family crest."

Their family crest.

Because of course his family would have a crest.

He grabs the knob, twisting it, then steps back and motions me into the apartment.

I've never been in this unit, but it takes only a step to know it's the best in the building, even fancier and *much* larger than Henrietta's. The marble floor in the foyer is the deepest, most vibrant green I've ever seen. Beside us, a stone fountain—four feet across, at least—trickles water from a lion's head. Ahead,

Grecian columns—similar to the enormous ones in the dining room—hold up an archway that must be twenty feet tall.

And as I follow Malik into the living room, my gaze goes up, up, up. The windows soar to the high ceiling, letting in a swath of light. And, thanks to being at the center of the building, they angle toward the point, almost like the bow of a ship, and I can finally see the lake in both directions. I can see the I-90 floating bridge spanning Lake Washington and, in the distance, the skyscrapers of Seattle.

"Wow," I say, unable to take my eyes off the windows. Henrietta has a great view, but the extra ninety degrees here really show why this suite rents for top dollar and is considered the best in the building. "This is—"

"Who are you?" someone barks.

I whirl around, realizing I'd been so distracted by the view that I walked right past the apartment's occupant.

Charles Buchannan is sitting at one end of an enormous button-back Chesterfield leather sofa, glaring at me so hard, his eyes have become two narrow slits. My mouth goes dry. I shouldn't be here. I should be—

"Grandpa, this is Lucy. Her . . ." Malik pauses and looks at me. "Your grandma?"

"Uh, what?" I ask, except I think it comes out more like muffled nonsense because I can barely breathe and there's definitely a lump in my throat. Why did I think this was a good idea? Charles Buchannan looks really, epically mad at me for setting foot in here.

"Henrietta. Is she your Grandma? Aunt?"

"Oh." *Breathe, Holly.* "Yes."

"Which one?"

I swallow, glancing over at Mr. Buchannan. I want to say *neither*, explain who I really am, but I can't just blurt it out now. Mr. Buchannan looks like he wants to shoot daggers at me with his eyes.

I'll explain the whole thing to Malik later. If there even is a later. "Um, Grandma."

Malik turns back to Mr. Buchannan. "Her grandma lives two doors down."

"So?" he snarls, crossing his arms. If body language were words, his would be *get out of my apartment*. "What's she doing here?"

"She's my friend," Malik says simply. His words make the blush creep back in, and I look away, my eyes trailing over the furniture in the room. He has exquisite taste—a Tiffany lamp sits on a Chippendale sideboard, a bronze sculpture perches on a pedestal near the window, and a pair of French Renaissance, glass-front bookcases sits opposite the couch, stuffed full of leather-bound books.

And then my gaze falls on a painting hanging high over the books. "*The Clothed Maja*," I say, my awe obvious. The painting had hung in the Prado Museum for over a century, until they finally sold it just a few years ago. I step closer to it, blinking as if it'll disappear. Or maybe turn into a regular print. A reproduction.

If Malik is a lifeboat on the *Titanic*, this painting is something better. It's so amazing, I'd go down with the ship just to stay close to it.

The room falls silent, and I return my eyes to Mr. Buchannan, who's staring at me with an unreadable expression, his eyes dark, his lips pursed.

"I mean, sorry, I don't mean to—"

"It is," he says, sitting back in his chair, the tightness in his crossed arms loosening up, like I've dented his armor. "Picked it up at the Prado auction two years ago."

"You were the phone bidder," I say, my eyes widening. I'd read all about it on one of my favorite design blogs—the phone bidder's identity had been debated and discussed, become the thing of legends overnight.

His lips twitch and I swear he's almost smiling, which is impossible. I've seen his face in the papers, on the evening news, and he never smiles. His face could be chiseled into Mt. Rushmore or put on a penny or something, it's so permanently stoic.

I look up at the painting again, studying the light and dark, the curves of the woman's body on canvas. "Its partner is here in Seattle, you know."

He says nothing. I flick a glance over at him and he's frozen. I don't know if he's stunned or confused. *The Nude Maja?*" I add.

Unlike Mr. Buchannan's painting, *The Nude Maja* had been sold privately, moments before the auction. It was never explained why, and everyone hoped the same person had purchased both pieces, at least at first. They belonged together, after all. Separating them was tragic.

"I know what *The Nude Maja* is," he snaps.

Okay, then. I glance back up at the painting on the wall, racking my brains to bring up everything I know about the artwork. The two paintings, by a Spanish painter named Francisco Goya, are a matched pair. They're over two hundred years old and feature the same model in the same pose—but in one she's clothed, and in the other, she's nude.

"But it's not in Seattle," he says. "I would have heard about it."

"I mean, maybe I'm wrong," I say, glancing over at Malik, waiting for him to bail me out.

Instead, he's got his head tipped to the side and is staring at his grandfather like he's trying to figure out a puzzle, like this conversation has surprised him. Is it weird that I'm talking to his grandfather? Or weird that *he's* talking to me?

I clear my throat. "I, uh, saw it on this design blog I follow, in the comments. Someone claimed it's going to be the show-piece in some auction next month."

"Show me."

"Show you the painting?" I dart another glance over at Malik. He crosses his arms and shrugs. "Um, it's part of an estate—"

"The blog, girl!" he says, throwing up his hands in exaspera-tion. "Show me the blog."

"Oh! Uh . . ." I swallow, suddenly feeling entirely in over my head. I should have just kept my mouth shut. Or never walked into this apartment. My mom is going to totally flip when she realizes I've been in here, getting Mr. Buchannan all riled up. "I mean, I don't have my laptop with me."

"You can use his iPad," Malik says, finally chiming in. He strides into an adjacent room, leaving me alone with his grand-father for an awkward, painfully silent moment, before return-ing with the tablet.

"Um, okay. Yeah, sure."

I pop open the browser and Google the name of the blog. At first I can't find the mention of the *The Nude Maja* in the last few posts, and my heart starts a steady climb up my throat, picturing the snarly face of Mr. Buchannan and the moment he decides I'm a total idiot.

But then it's there, buried four posts down, in the comments trail.

"Here," I say, walking to him with the iPad held out. "Some guy named Roger Cartwell passed away—"

"Cartwell!" he exclaims. "Cartwell had it the whole time?"

I swallow. "Um, well, I guess it was in his collection. Mozak and Klein are scheduled to handle the auction next month, but they haven't put out any press."

"We're going there," he says, abruptly standing. "You two can take me."

I'm so stunned, I hardly move, just grip the iPad and stare at him, slack-jawed. When he steps past me, leaning on a cane and muttering something about his coat, I finally snap my mouth shut.

Malik meets my gaze, his eyes flared wide in surprise, before grabbing his grandfather's jacket off a nearby wingback chair.

"Uh," I say, feeling as if I'm in the eye of a storm and everything is spinning out of control. "I mean, it's not like I know where he lives."

"I do," Mr. Buchannan says, slipping his arms into the jacket when Malik holds it out. "Went to a fundraiser at his house two years ago. Should have known that man would have *The Nude Maja* and not tell me about it." He limps his way to the foyer.

"He *knew* I had its match. It would probably kill him to see it in my hands."

He pauses at the door, flashing the first real, toothy smile I've ever seen on his face. "Lucky for me, he's already dead!"

And then he disappears out the door. I'm about to follow him into the hall when Malik stops me, a hand on my arm.

A wide grin envelops his face. "He hasn't left home voluntarily in months."

"Oh?" I say, barely able to speak. My mouth is dry. I need water. I need . . . the Bering freaking Sea.

"Yeah. I'm so happy, I could kiss you."

And then he spins on his heel and hustles after Mr. Buchannan.

I scramble to follow, Malik's words ringing in my ears.

CHAPTER FOUR

Malik drives like a professional race-car driver. I'm glad I can't actually see the speedometer because I'm a little worried about how fast we're going. Occasionally, he glances up at me in the rearview mirror, and I catch a glimpse of one deep brown eye and that perfectly styled eyebrow, and it reminds me just how acutely out of place I am, sitting in the backseat of his luxury car, in my flowy pink cotton shirt I sewed out of some discarded drapes and blue jeans I picked up at Sears.

Sears. I shop at Sears. I bet if I told Malik that, he'd kick me out of the car for fear the cheap fabric could scuff his pricy leather seats.

"Thank god we're finally out of that place," Mr. Buchannan grumbles beneath his breath.

Malik darts a glance at his grandfather, and I wonder if he's thinking the same thing I am—that apparently Mr. Buchannan never wants to go anywhere in the first place. "If you wanted to get out and do something—"

"I don't want to *go* anywhere, I just need to get away from that silly manager."

"Mrs. Weaver? She seemed—"

"No. The other one. Miranda something-or-other."

I nearly gulp aloud, shrinking into my seat. People always say my mother and I look alike.

"Oh, come on, she's not that bad," Malik offers. "She seemed pretty nice when I met her yesterday."

"She's constantly trying to get me into all those stupid activities! It's not even her job, you know. I saw her business card. She's a leasing specialist. She leased me the place; what business is it of hers if I partake of those stupid activities?" He hits the door with his fist. "It's not as if I'm going to sit around playing bingo! Does she even know who I am? What I've accomplished? Why would I play *bingo*?"

The air is suddenly too hot and stuffy, and I crack the window, but it doesn't help; it just seems to draw attention to the fact that I'm back here.

"Mr. Buchannan," I say, my voice coming out unsure and wobbly. "Uh, I'm sure she's just trying to be helpful. My, um, grandma really likes her. She's really a wonderful person. Sometimes she sits in the café with my grandma and they read the Sunday paper together."

Malik meets my eyes, and our gazes lock. I get the feeling he's trying to say *thank you*. "Yeah, just let her do her job, Grandpa."

Just don't make her lose her job, Gramps. She needs it. I need it.

"She needs to leave me alone, is what she needs to do." Before the conversation can go further, Mr. Buchannan points to an upcoming road, and Malik slows just enough that the tires don't squeal as we round the corner. I keep waiting for his grandpa to tell him to slow down, but he seems oblivious of the speed, or maybe he's just that eager to see the art.

"This one on the right," he says, pointing to a house hidden behind a tall brick wall. "Pull up to the gatehouse."

Malik downshifts, slowing to a stop next to the little building near the front gates. A security guard steps out, waving the car down.

Of course these people hang out at homes with gatehouses and security guards. This is normal to them. They probably have a vault and they swim in their gold coins every day and they've got to keep the riffraff out somehow, so they install guards and gatehouses and those laser security systems with ninety-seven beams only a gymnast or Charlize Theron could avoid.

Malik rolls his window down, and his grandpa leans across the center console.

"Can I help you?" the guard asks.

"We're here for *The Nude Maja*."

He narrows his eyes. "I don't know what that is, Mr. . . .?"

"Buchannan. Charles Buchannan. And it's a painting."

Surprise flashes across the guard's face as it sinks in just who is sitting at his gate. "Mr. Buchannan," he says, his tone now sweet and accommodating. "Pleased to meet you. But I'm sorry, sir, the auction isn't until next month."

"I don't want to wait. Surely you can allow me to speak with someone."

He pauses, studying Mr. Buchannan and then glancing back at the house again. "Just give me a moment."

He retreats to his desk, and we watch in silence as he picks up a phone. Two minutes later a buzz rings out and the gate swings open.

"Go ahead on up to the house. Ms. Cartwell is in. She'll talk to you."

"Thanks," Malik says before taking off, the tires chirping. The engine purrs as we cruise up the circular drive, then park next to a big copper sculpture. It sort of resembles a bird, except it's basically the size of a dinosaur.

When Mr. Buchannan slams his door, I realize I'm just sitting in the backseat, gawking, and Malik is waiting for me to slide out from behind his seat.

I climb out, staring in awe at the house before me. It's shockingly modern, all ninety-degree angles and walls of glass, giant steel beams holding it all together. Like a series of boxes stacked on top of one another, the upper floor sort of cantilevers over the bottom one. One side of the house is completely see-through—you can even see the lake on the other side.

I try not to show my astonishment, since I know Malik probably lives in a house like this—or even swankier—but it's hard not to.

As I finally stop gawking, the front door of the house swings open and a woman in her fifties, dressed smartly in a navy wrap dress and heels, steps out into the sunshine. She's so poised and glamorous that she looks like she could be the first lady or something.

"I think that's Cartwell's daughter," Malik whispers, leaning over so close, his breath is hot on my ear.

Panic shoots through me. Malik may not notice my clothes, but surely this fashionable lady is going to ask who the heck I am and why I shop at Goodwill.

I shouldn't have come with them. I should've faked a sudden headache.

"Mr. Buchannan, what a surprise," she says, smiling as she shakes his hand. "We met years ago, at the Fifth Avenue Theater. What brings you to the house?"

"I want *The Nude Maja*," he says, but it comes out more like a bark. This man is nothing if not to the point. I can picture him now in his boardroom, commanding a roomful of people in thousand-dollar suits.

She blinks. "I'm afraid you'll have to wait for the auction," she says. "It's our centerpiece."

"I'll give you four million," he says. "Probably more than it'll fetch. It's more than I paid for *The Clothed Maja* at the Prado sale."

She pauses, and I think I choke on my spit.

FOUR MILLION DOLLARS? Just like that?

She recovers, flashing him an empty smile. "I'm sorry, but without the painting, we may get fewer attendees. I need it to headline the sale. Mozak and Klein said—"

"Five," he says.

She snaps her mouth shut, studying him. Sizing him up.

Seconds tick by, and it starts to feel like a showdown at the OK Corral. "Let me call Mozak and Klein and ask . . ."

"Can we see it?" Malik asks, stepping forward. "The painting, that is. I'd like to know what all the fuss is about."

She turns, as if just noticing the two of us. Her eyes dart between me and Malik, but if she's surprised by my presence, or my attire, she doesn't show it. "Why not? Come on in, and I'll call Mozak and Klein while you take a look at the collection. It'll just take a moment."

We follow her up the steps and into the home. We find ourselves in a giant open great room, big enough to play basketball or rugby or something in. What I didn't see from outside, thanks to the glare of the afternoon sun, is that it's filled with folding tables covered with sculptures and lamps and jewelry boxes. As I watch Ms. Cartwell pick up her cell phone off a table and head out of the room, I notice that, along one wall, two dozen easels prop up a variety of colorful paintings.

I scan the room, looking for the Goya, but I make it just three easels down before I stop.

"A Volpi," I say, pointing to the third painting. I'm not even a little bit embarrassed by the breathiness of my voice. A Volpi calls for shock and awe. "It's beautiful."

I step farther into the room, my eyes wandering over the most exquisite collection I've ever seen.

Mr. Buchannan walks right past me, to the last easel. To the Goya. He freezes there, staring, his body blocking the painting from my view. Even though I want to see it, it feels oddly . . . intimate. Private. Like he's spent his lifetime in search of this one painting, and he can't believe he's so close to it.

I turn away, studying the next painting. "And a Pollock," I say. "I can't believe one person has all this."

Malik stops in front of the Pollack, studying the canvas. "How do you know this stuff?"

I smile at him. "When I was a baby, my grandma gave my mom an antique rocking chair. It'd been in the family a long time and it was really pretty, with carvings on the armrests and seatback." I pause, realizing he's going to assume that the grandmother I'm referring to is Henrietta, not my mother's mom, who passed away ten years ago. I guess it doesn't matter. "I loved it as a little kid just because it had a seat cushion with teddy bears on it. Something she'd sewed herself. My mom put it in my room and no matter how many times we moved, the chair always came with us. It kind of became this one stable thing in my life."

"You moved a lot growing up?"

My breath hitches in my throat as I realize how much truth I've shared with him. Wealthy people don't schlep from one place to another, not like we did. "Um, yeah, my mom was, you know, climbing the career ladder."

Understatement of the year.

"By the time I was ten or twelve, it was like I started to recognize how when things are made well, they last. And I started seeing that in other things, and becoming more fascinated. I guess it was all downhill from there. To me, antiques . . . fine art . . . they're a symbol of something, you know? Permanence, I guess. Plus, I like the way everything used to be built by hand. I like to picture the artist at his canvas or the furniture maker sculpting the trim on a table leg, turning it by hand, sanding it hour after hour."

I don't tell him how part of me loves these things because they have stood the test of time, and all I ever had growing up was the cheapest of everything, stuff that broke constantly.

There's a *click-click-clack* as Ms. Cartwell returns, her cell dangling from her fingers. Malik and I turn around, and I know instantly by the thin line of her lips that it's not good news. "I'm sorry, Mr. Buchannan. They were clear that we need Goya's painting to headline the sale. Without it, we'll attract a fraction of the buyers. Even if they pay less for the Goya than you've offered, it's worth it to have it in the sale."

"How much?" Mr. Buchannan says.

She crosses her arms. "I'm sorry. You'll have to wait for the auction to buy the painting."

"Not the Goya, woman," he says, crossing his own arms. As if it's a contest or something. "For all of it."

I can't help but take a step back, shocked, and I bump into Malik. He grips my elbows, keeping me from knocking both of us to the ground.

She raises a brow. "You want to buy everything in this room?"

"Yes."

She darts a glance over at Malik and me, like we're going to rein him in or something. Obviously, she doesn't know I'm a total stranger. "Mozak and Klein estimated twelve million for the collection," she says.

"Done. Cancel the sale."

She's stunned, simply staring at Mr. Buchannan as if he's grown a second head.

He just spent twelve million dollars.

Twelve.

Million.

Dollars.

He walks to the table and picks up a clipboard that some-one's left behind, quickly scribbling something down before handing it to her. "Have it all shipped to this address. I'd like it within a week. My banker's phone number is at the bottom. I'll authorize the wire transfer. Just give him your information."

He pauses. "And I'm taking *The Nude Maja* with me. Malik?"

Malik nods, seemingly unfazed by his grandfather's shop-ping spree. He walks to the painting and stops just shy of it. "Do you have some kind of packing crate?"

"It's going straight up on my wall," Mr. Buchannan says. "Just don't drive quite like you did on the way here and it'll sur-vive a trip in the backseat with Lucy."

Moments later, we're walking back to the car. It could just be me, but I swear Mr. Buchannan has serious bounce in his step. I also think he's humming beneath his breath, but it's too faint to know for sure. It's like he's not even the same person.

Malik slides the painting into the backseat next to me and then climbs into the front seat and we're off.

I'm sitting in the backseat of a silver sports car, next to a two-hundred-year-old Spanish painting, with one of the richest men on earth in the passenger seat and the hottest boy I've ever met behind the wheel.

And they both think my name is Lucy.

CHAPTER FIVE

Twenty minutes later, Malik hands his keys off to a valet at Sunrise House and rounds the car, meeting me where I'm sliding out from behind the passenger seat. I step to the side, and he gently slides the painting out, inspecting the frame and canvas as if to make sure it survived the trip.

"I don't have all day," Mr. Buchannan calls out.

I glance over Malik's shoulder, realizing Mr. Buchannan is already at the front entryway to Sunrise House, leaning on his cane. The way he's acting, you'd think he was a little kid waiting to open up his birthday present.

"The maintenance guys are around until six, if you want them to hang that," I say. And then my heart shoots up to my throat. "I mean, I think so, anyway. I called them once for Henrietta."

"Cool," Malik says. "You coming up with us?"

The front door of his car slams shut, and I realize the valet is ready to go park it, so I step away, shutting the back door. "Um, no, I really can't. I'm just going to pick up a treat at the bakery for Henrietta and then I've got to get home."

It's not true, but I'm sure my mom is wondering where the heck I got off to, and I can't just walk straight to my apartment with Malik watching.

"You sure?" he says, nodding toward the painting. "You don't want to see the art version of a family reunion?"

I grin, and temptation swells. *Soon.* I'll see them soon. I can come up with some reason to swing by Mr. Buchannan's place. "Maybe some other time?"

"Sure. Text me so I'll have your number," he says, and then starts rattling off his phone number.

"Oh, um, hold on," I say, digging my phone out of my pocket and willing myself not to jump up and down and squeal.

Malik is giving me his phone number.

MALIK IS GIVING ME HIS PHONE NUMBER!

"Okay, got it," I say a moment later, clicking Send on my phone.

"Cool," he says. "Maybe we can go out soon. . . ."

"Sometime today, kid!" Mr. Buchannan calls.

Malik laughs under his breath. "Later, I guess," he says, turning away to follow his very impatient grandfather. "Text me."

"Okay. Yeah. Definitely." I enter Sunrise House, feeling like I'm floating on air as I walk in the opposite direction as Malik, toward the bakery, until they step into the elevator and disappear.

Then I make a U-Turn and head to my apartment, which is only a few doors past the elevator, not far from the billiards room. Which I can now pass in peace, by the way, since the sofa is in the right location.

The apartment is quiet when I slip inside, and I'm relieved. I half expected it to be like one of those clichéd scenes in a movie where the parents are sitting on the couch and they go *Where have you been all night?* when the kid walks in.

In the kitchen, I dig a tub of salsa from the fridge and rip open a fresh bag of tortilla chips.

I'm just dipping a chip into some salsa when my mom walks in.

"Where did you go with Charles Buchannan?"

I freeze mid-scoop. "What?"

"You signed him out at the front desk," she says, and I don't miss the edge of nerves in her voice. "I saw it. Only relatives are supposed to do that. Where did you take him?"

"Ohhhhh," I say as my stomach dances a painful jig. Malik had walked right past the sign-out book, and I'd been worried everyone would think Charles went missing, so I'd scribbled him out myself. I blurt out the first thing I can think of. "The circus."

She rolls her eyes. "For real, Holly."

"Um, the park?" I ask, trying to decide if the truth is worse than fiction.

"You've never been a good liar," she says, hanging her building keys up on a hook near the door.

Hahaha, that's hilarious. I'm a way better liar than she thinks I am.

I swallow. "Ummmmmmmmmmmmmmm," I say, stretching the word out so long, it could be seven syllables. Then, realizing

I'm still standing there holding one freaking chip, I stuff it into my mouth.

"You're making me nervous."

Right. Of course I am. Everything about Charles makes my mom nervous. She's going to freak out when she realizes I spent the afternoon with him!

"We went for a drive," I say around the chip. I mean, it's not my fault he spent twelve million dollars, right? Plus he's a bajillionaire, so it's pretty much the same thing as twelve dollars to him.

My mom can't get in trouble for it, right?

I think. I mean, he's a senior citizen and some of them *do* have restrictions like that in place, but it's not stuff my mom is responsible for seeing through. One of the residents is such a shopaholic, she's not even allowed to have her credit cards in her room, but she keeps ordering new ones and then someone always has to intercept her mail.

"You drove him around town?"

"Not exactly," I say, swirling another chip around in the salsa.

"How do you *not exactly* drive him around?"

"His grandson was the one driving," I say, trying to swallow the chip. It feels like it turned sideways in my throat.

"Grandson?"

I take a swig of water, finally meeting her eyes. "Uh-huh. His name is Malik. I met him yesterday. He's nice. Around my age."

"And they just . . . invited you on a drive," she says in such a way that I know she's waiting for the other shoe to drop.

"Yeah."

"Where did you go?"

I lean a hip against the counter. "To Roger Cartwell's house."

"Who?"

"Some guy who died."

"Why?" she says, her voice growing exasperated, like she just wants to say, *Out with it already.*

"To buy art," I say, as if I'm talking about a reprint at Target. "You know, for his new place. All those blank walls and everything. . . ."

But she's not buying it and searches my eyes for the real answer. "You went with Charles Buchannan to someone's house to buy art. A man who has not voluntarily gone on any excursion of any kind in months."

I give her a little jazz hands, like I just performed a magic trick. She wanted him to get out of Sunrise House, right? "Yep."

"And what happened?"

Oh. Right. Not magic. I quit the silly grin and steeple my hands in mock-prayer. "Please don't be mad. I couldn't say no. One minute I was admiring his Goya painting, and the next we're zipping across the bridge."

"Did he get it?"

"Get what?"

"The art."

"Oh. Yeah. Actually he bought the guy's whole collection. For . . ." I trail off and mumble the last part.

"For what?"

"Twelve million," I say, louder this time. "I went with Charles Buchannan to some fancy estate to buy twelve million dollars' worth of art."

She's so stunned, she says nothing, just stares.

"I know."

"You invited yourself, didn't you? You heard about the art and you couldn't resist the idea of seeing—"

"No," I say, throwing up my hands to stop her. "He invited me, I swear. I wasn't an intrusion. I barely said a word the whole time."

"I should go talk to him. Make sure he's not upset," she says. "I'm not sure why he'd want my teenage daughter accompanying him on that kind of a trip, especially if he's been reclusive for so long."

"Wait, I'm not in trouble? I thought you'd flip. I'm not allowed to sign residents out."

"No, I'm not mad," she says, walking to the fridge to grab a bottle of water.

I study her, taking in her relaxed posture, the casual way she twists open the water.

"There's something you're not telling me," I say.

"What?"

"You nearly grounded me last month for walking Henrietta down the block without approval. I went miles away with Mr. Buchannan. Why aren't you ticked?"

Condensation trails over my mom's fingertips as she twists the lid back on. "His daughter just called. That's why I came to find you."

"The one who set him up here?"

She nods. "Yeah. Her son—Malik, I assume—texted her that Mr. Buchannan voluntarily left his apartment, and she was thrilled. I had no idea what she was talking about, of course, so

I played along until I could open the logbook, and then I saw your name."

I grin widely. "So, you're telling me I scored you brownie points? Sweet."

She waggles a finger at me. "Not so fast, missy. Her enthusiasm will fade if you annoyed him with your little tagalong adventure and he never leaves again. I still have to talk to him."

"You can't," I say, walking closer to her.

"Why?"

"He doesn't know we're related," I say. "And, um, he kind of grumbled about you? I didn't know what to do, and I sorta came to your defense, and if you out me now, he's going to know I was biased and think we were trying to trick him or something and . . . well, you know. He seems like he's the suspicious sort."

"You didn't tell him you're my daughter?"

"No."

And he doesn't know my name is Holly.

"So either I tell him, and he feels like you were dishonest with him, or I don't, and we risk his finding out later and thinking the same thing."

"Yeah. But you know, he might not find out, and I'm going to college in, like, two months, so I don't think it's a big deal."

She runs a hand through her hair, looking like this bit of news deflated her a little. "We can't lose him as a resident, Holly. You have no idea how thrilled Mrs. Weaver was that I filled that unit. If he moves in one week and then I drive him away the next, I could get fired."

"I know."

She chews on her lip. "I guess you're right. You'll be gone before we know it," she points out, tapping her nails on the countertop.

"Yeah. I mean, I'll be six hours away."

"Okay. Then we won't tell him," she says. "But avoid him as much as possible until you head off to school."

"Okay," I say.

"I mean it, Holly. Stay away from Charles Buchannan."

"Scout's honor," I say, giving her the little two-finger salute.

I can avoid Charles.

But she didn't say anything about Malik.

CHAPTER SIX

Meet me at the rain garden at Redmond Town Center at 7.
I'm taking you out.

That's all Malik's text says. I guess I shouldn't be surprised;
the boy is used to getting what he wants. I bet he's never had a
girl refuse him. Not that I'm going to be that girl, or anything.
After a few days of silence, I thought maybe he'd forgotten all
about me. So, basically, my heart has been dancing a jig since
the text arrived.

Also, my room looks like it's been hit by a hurricane.

I have nothing to wear. My clothes are all old and faded and
worn and stretched and cheap and . . .

I have nothing to wear.

"ARGH!" I scream in frustration, throwing the last piece of
clothing over my shoulder to land on the pile on my bed. I wrack
my brains for some scrap of clothing that might be unaccounted

for. That might be hidden under my bed or in the washing machine or something.

I don't know why I'm freaking out. Malik has seen my less-than-stellar clothes already. But this . . . this is different. This is supposed to be a *date*. Romantic and special and . . .

I blow out a slow breath.

"Whoa," a voice says. I spin around to find my mom standing in the doorway, surveying the damage. "Uh, spring cleaning?"

I grimace. "I have a date and I have nothing to wear."

She narrows her eyes. "Is this a group thing, or a—"

"No, just the two of us."

"And who is the lucky guy?"

I stare at the carpet, burrowing my toes in. "Don't be mad."

"Why would I be mad?"

"It's Malik Buchannan."

"Oh," she says, and when I glance up her lips are parted, her eyes wide with surprise.

And I know, without a doubt, the Malik she's picturing is the one everyone else sees. The billionaire's playboy grandson. The heir to a kingdom.

"Yeah. But I swear I won't talk about you at all, and we're meeting in Redmond, so I won't see his grandpa or anything. *Please, please, please* let me go."

She studies me, and I can see her churning through all the possibilities, wondering if this is a bad idea. For effect, I drop to my knees. "Please, please, please?"

She crosses her arms, leaning against the doorjamb. "Fine. I guess it's okay as long as his grandfather isn't around."

"Really?" I ask, surprised.

"I don't like it," she says, "but I have a feeling warning you away won't do me much good. So just . . . be careful."

"I won't hang out with him here at all," I say. "I'll stay away from Mr. Buchannan just like we said."

"That's not what I meant," she says.

"Oh."

"I meant . . . just don't get hurt by *him*. Malik. I understand he's dated a long list of girls. I don't know that you want to invest much of yourself in the relationship."

"He's not the guy on TMZ," I say. "He's . . . nice. I think I can trust him."

It's like she's fighting the urge to roll her eyes. "I thought I could trust your father, and look how that turned out."

I grit my teeth. "Geez, he's not Dad, Mom. He's a good guy. And we're not serious. It's just one date."

"All right then. If you're going to do this, I guess I could loan you an outfit."

"Really?" I ask, brightening. I can't believe she's cool with this.

"Yeah. It's just a date, right? You're still going off to college soon."

It hits me, then, that she can't fathom the idea that anything between Malik and me could be real or could become serious.

She's letting me do this because she thinks nothing will come of it.

It's a fling. And that's a good thing, because if it's only a fling, maybe I don't have to tell Malik who I really am. Where I come from. We can have fun this summer and then just . . . move on, and he'll never know my real name.

"Right," I say, because it's the only rational answer. "We're just hanging out."

She sighs, and I have the strongest feeling she's giving in to this, despite her better instincts. "I have a skirt. It's too small so I was going to return it, but it would go nicely with that blouse," she says, pointing to a pale pink sleeveless V-neck on my bed.

"Perfect."

I follow her over to her room, and she steps into her enormous walk-in closet, returning with a black pencil skirt, a pair of heels dangling from her fingertips. "Try this."

I grin and bounce forward, giving her a quick hug. "Thank you, thank you, thank you."

"Just don't make me regret it, okay? I think I'm finally winning over Charles."

"Really?"

She nods. "Or maybe just wearing him down. I procured a promise that he would consider trying one of the restaurants. I don't know—maybe he was just saying it to get rid of me. So far he's only done meal delivery."

"Wow," I say. "That's good."

"Yeah. Hopefully, he follows through. Maybe you can figure out how to plant a bug in Malik's ear, get him to convince Charles to go sooner rather than later."

"I'll do my best," I say. "I kind of sensed some tension between them. I don't think he appreciates that his daughter and grandson keep pushing him."

"Well, maybe I'll figure out how to lure him out on my own."

"Good luck," I say, stepping out of her bedroom. "And thanks for the clothes."

• • •

Two hours later, I'm standing beside the rain garden in Redmond Town Center, watching three kids whoop and holler and smack everything they can find with rubber mallets. I've never been here before, but according to the placard, the usual Seattle rain is supposed to make a bunch of different noises when it hits the various metal domes and cones and iron leaves.

Only, it's the kids, their hands, and the mallets smacking all the surfaces who create a surprisingly pleasant melody on this dry summer night.

Trying not to check the time on my phone for the millionth time today, I pick up a nearby mallet, which is dangling from a short cable, and smack it on a steel xylophone.

The notes are marked on the keys, like it's an eight-year-old's piano, and after a couple of leisurely whacks, I find myself tapping out the tune to "Oh Susanna," the one I learned how to play on a plastic recorder in sixth-grade music class.

"Wow, gorgeous *and* musically talented. How did I ever get so lucky?"

I spin around, dropping the mallet. It bangs against the keys, then clatters against the iron railing surrounding the rain garden. "You're late," I say, because it's the first thing that comes to mind.

"Sorry. Traffic was a little rough. But I promise we haven't missed the movie."

"Oh," I say, because I didn't even know we were seeing a movie. This really is a *date* date.

As I scramble to say something else, something intelligent or witty or just *something*, Malik grabs my hand, leading me away from the clattering and chiming of the rain garden.

"I thought we could go for an action flick, if you're up for it," he says as we approach the staircase that will lead us to the second floor of the outdoor shopping center. "Or you can pick something else."

"No, that sounds perfect," I say, squeezing his hand. It's still . . . surreal to be with him right now. On an official, let's-go-see-a-movie kind of date. Maybe I'm the sort of girl who stars in romantic movies after all.

"Great."

We cross the walkway and arrive at a theater. But Malik doesn't stop at the box office to buy tickets. Instead, he just walks right past it and leads me through a set of double doors.

Inside, there's a line of patrons and a guy in a black vest standing at a big wooden podium. Malik just steps around the line, tugging me past vest-guy.

The guy nods, as if he's expecting us, and lets us pass without flashing any tickets. Is this how it works when you're rich or famous or something? People just . . . let you walk into a movie theater and no one expects you to pay?

I mean, I always heard that saying about how once you're rich enough to pay for things, people want to give them to you for free. But I thought that applied to, like, Versace gowns for the VMAs or something.

Malik speed-walks through the lobby, passing by the popcorn and soda and everything else. But I don't tug him to a stop, despite my sudden and earth-shattering need for buttery, salty popcorn. He's a man on a mission, and I'm not sure where the sense of urgency is coming from. Maybe he doesn't want to be recognized. Or maybe he just doesn't like movie theater popcorn. Which would be his one tragic flaw, and this whole relationship is doomed from the start, because I don't know if I can be with a boy who doesn't like movie theater popcorn.

We round a corner, where a pair of double doors are propped open, and a fresh wave of buttery aroma greets me. It's only when he pulls me inside, and two vested workers close the doors behind us, that I know why.

There is a snack station set up on a rolling red cart inside the theater. Two tubs of popcorn, stacks of candy boxes, bottles of soda . . . It's like a diabetic coma. Except I've never seen a snack station like this, inside the actual theater. And I don't see the point if it's got only two tubs of popcorn. It's really only enough for a few people.

And then it hits me and I feel like an idiot. "Is this . . ."

"For us," he says.

I turn back to him, looking over his shoulder and realizing the entire theater is empty.

"Um, like . . . everything?"

"Yes. We have the theater to ourselves this evening."

Stunned, I simply stare, *Holy crap* running through my head over and over. "You . . . you rented out the whole theater?"

"Sort of," he says, enjoying my shock. "I called in a favor."

"What kind of a favor?"

He laughs. "A few weeks ago, I helped a board member's wife with the publicity for a charity 5K. She owns the theater."

"Oh." I glance around, still having trouble processing. "And this is really all just for the two of us?"

"Yes." His grin widens, turns almost smug. He's clearly enjoying my reaction—that I'm reeling from his reveal.

"We'll start the movie momentarily," one of the workers cuts in. "Skipping the previews, as you've requested, of course."

"No," I say, before I can stop myself.

"No?" Malik raises a brow. "You want to see them?"

"Yeah. I mean, I like the previews. I always pick out one movie I'm going to come back and see. My friend Alex and I always make a pact."

"Oh." He turns to the vested guy. "Um, yes, please play the previews."

"Okay, then," the guy says. "I'll get it set up. Please sit anywhere you'd like."

And then the workers step away and it's just me and Malik in the not-yet-dark theater.

"I can't believe you don't like the previews," I say, turning to the snack cart and surveying the options. "I bet you like to sit in the way back, too."

"Is that frowned upon?"

"Everyone knows the middle of the theater is best," I say, reaching for a box of Mike and Ikes and a tub of popcorn. "Middle row, middle seat."

"Lucky for you, you can have any seat you want," he says, grabbing a box of M&Ms.

He follows me down the aisle until I pause, glancing back and forth to be sure it's the exact middle row. When I'm satisfied, I walk down, stopping in the middle to count the seats on either side. Then I shift down one more spot and plunk myself into the most perfectly centered seat in the whole room.

The lights go down the moment I sit, as if someone upstairs has been anticipating this very moment, and the surreality of it hits me all over again.

I'm in an actual movie theater, but it's a private date.

The screen lights up, and Malik wraps his arm around my shoulders. With confidence, though, not like those dorky yawn-and-stretch maneuvers. More like he can't imagine a scenario in which a girl doesn't melt into his embrace.

Which isn't so far from the truth. I lean into him, resting my head back a bit and inhaling that same cinnamon scent I'd noticed the first day we met. I'm not sure if it's his cologne or his shampoo or what, but I hope he never changes it.

"So, you like shopping for movies from the previews, huh?"

"It's a rule Alex and I have. She's been my best friend since forever. We always pick the next movie we'll see together that way. For everything else, we wait for it to come out for download and we watch them at her house."

"Oh. Does this mean I've completely thrown off your system?"

I grin, glancing up at him as the first preview rolls, something exploding on screen. "I think I can find it in my heart to forgive you."

Two and a half hours later, I pull into the parking garage at Sunrise House, my car coughing and sputtering to a stop.

I wonder if Malik thought I was a total weirdo for insisting I needed to shop for a new fleece jacket at the mall at nine p.m. and that he absolutely, positively could not go with me.

It's just . . . until our date was over, it hadn't occurred to me he'd try to walk me to the car. So instead of saying good-bye in the parking lot, he hugged me good-bye under the glowing neon of a shop sign. I think he knew something was off, but he couldn't quite call me out on it.

I put my car in park and pick up my phone, hitting Alex's number on speed dial.

It rings four times and goes to voice mail.

"Ugh," I say, climbing out of my car and dialing again. She has to be at home. I need to tell her about tonight. She's never far from her phone. I hit Call again, pressing the phone to my ear as I leave my car behind, not bothering to lock it. It's the worst car in this whole place.

"Hello?" she asks on the third ring.

"Hey, it's me."

"I know, silly," she says.

"Oh. Right," I say. "Sorry. I'm a little all over the place right now."

"Why? What's up?"

"Um, I went on a date with Malik today. A real one."

"Seriously?" Her voice brightens.

"Yeah. I called you hours ago so you could give me some advice . . . but you haven't been picking up."

"Oh, gosh, sorry, Holls. My phone was dead for a while. Couldn't find the charger."

Lies. It would've gone straight to voice mail if it was shut off. I pause, processing that Alex clearly not only didn't want to pick up the phone but also is willing to lie about it, and try to ignore the painful twist in my stomach.

"So . . . how'd the date go?"

I blink, remembering why I'd wanted to talk to her in the first place. I'll worry about why she's been avoiding me later.

"Um, so, it was pretty good," I say, but it comes out hesitant.

"What aren't you telling me?"

I chew on my lip, staying silent as I slide my badge against the readers at the door between the parking garage and the back hallway. There's a solid *thunk* as the doors unlock.

"Holly?"

"He rented out an entire theater," I say in a rush. "Well, I mean, I don't think he paid for it—he knows someone, or something, and so they let us have the whole theater to ourselves. And I think we had, like, three dedicated workers just to replenish the little snack cart they brought in. I probably consumed ten thousand calories by the end of the date."

"Whoa, really?"

"Yeah. It was so nuts. Like, I got up to use the restroom halfway through, and they freaking paused the movie for me."

"Holy smokes, that is the most amazing date I have ever heard of." There's a beat of silence, and then, "Wait a sec, you don't sound that excited. Did you not like it?"

I chew on my lip as I walk past the bakery and restaurants and pause outside of the theater. I don't know . . . Did I not like it? "It was just . . ."

"What?"

"Extravagant," I said. "It seemed really over the top, and it just got me thinking about how different we are. I mean, where do we even go from here?"

"I'm sure he doesn't think it was that big of a deal," she says. "He's trying to impress you."

"I know, but I almost . . ." I pause. I can't believe I'm about to say this. "I kind of wish he didn't."

"You don't want to be impressed?"

"Not like that," I say, looking up at the big chandelier outside of the theater. It's at least six feet tall, all ornate, curling brass. "It just has me feeling like my head is spinning."

"I can't believe you're complaining about this."

I rub a hand over my face. "Do you think I'm being ungrateful?"

"A little," she says. In the background, I can hear a voice. And then she clearly covers the mouthpiece, saying something muffled.

I blink. "Are you with someone?"

"Just Rena."

"Oh. Sorry," I say, suddenly feeling awkward. "Uh, I didn't mean to interrupt . . . whatever you guys are doing."

"No big," she says. "But I gotta get going. Sleep on it, and I bet you'll get over the shock and realize how awesome the date was."

"Yeah, maybe."

"I mean, *I* can't even believe he did that, and it wasn't for me. So you just need to . . . adjust . . . or something."

"Mm-hmm," I say, trying to decide what it is about the date that has me so flummoxed.

And then I realize it's not the date at all, but Malik.

It's the easy way he strolled in like he owned the place . . . the way they knew to skip the previews, the way he casually waved his hand to signal *pause the movie* and they did so in seconds. . . .

Like this date was nothing to him, just a blip on the radar.

If life is *really* that simple to him . . .

Then maybe I'm nothing, too. Just a tiny little blip. One he'll leave behind on a search for bigger and better things.

CHAPTER SEVEN

A few days later, I'm standing at the edge of the lake, my toes dipped in the gleaming blue water of Lake Washington. I'm dreaming up an alternate world, where I'm wearing Prada and Gucci and I'm standing beside Malik on a red carpet. And his is not the only name the photographers are calling out—they care who I am too.

The lake splashes up around my ankles as a gentle wave rolls in, caused by a passing yacht.

I wonder if Malik has a yacht. He probably does, and it's tied up back at Mr. Buchannan's lakefront mansion.

There are some yachts here, too. Sunrise House has a private marina, barely a hundred feet away from where I stand. There are only a half dozen slips, but some of the residents have boats moored there as part of their lease or whatever. My mom has been trying out all this ridiculous boat lingo so that she won't look like an idiot if she tries to use the moorage as a selling point to a potential new tenant.

I wonder what it would be like to spend the day on a big boat with Malik, sunbathing and drinking fancy sparkling water and eating grapes, or whatever rich people do. I'm so lost in outlandish daydreams of his endlessly deep, warm brown eyes, that when I hear his voice—hear him say, "Lucy"—I almost think I imagine it.

But then a shadow falls across the sand beside me, and I shield my eyes, looking up to meet his gaze. He's so tall and I'm so short, that from this angle the sun creates a halo around his head, casting his expression in shadow.

"Um, hey," I say, my heart thundering to life, like it, too, just woke from sleep. "What's up?"

Casual. I sound casual, right? And not like my insides are completely malfunctioning and I can't stop swallowing and I think the butterflies in my stomach are probably cannibals and attacking each other? Why does he always have this effect on me?

He stops a foot farther back from the waterline, to keep his leather shoes from getting wet. "You have plans this afternoon?"

"Uhh . . ." I glance back at Sunrise House. From here—across the grassy lawn, beyond the beautiful cedar trees and manicured hedges—it looks like it's in deep slumber. No sounds, no lights switching on or off, no faint music trickling out on a breeze.

I try to peer into my mom's office window to discern if she can see the two of us down here, but there's too much glare. And besides, I didn't tell her I was going for a walk, so she probably can't even tell it's me from this distance. "No?"

"Good. Then you can come with me."

"Where?"

No, not where. *Yes*, please*! I don't care if we're going to a Miley Cyrus concert.*

"My house."

The butterflies are climbing up my throat now. "Um, your house?"

"Yes. Well, it's my grandfather's house, really, but I've lived there for a year, so I guess it's home now."

"Oh," I say, finally breathing again. "Has the art arrived already?"

He digs at the sand with the toe of his leather shoe. "No, but he wants more furniture in his new place. I'm supposed to go tag it and have it picked up, but I don't know what would look good. And I figured, who better to ask than you?"

I cross my arms, smirking. "So, you're telling me you're not actually good at *everything*."

His smile reveals a perfectly straight row of bright white teeth. "*Almost* everything; furniture's not my gig. But you seem to have a good eye for this stuff. We can shop through the house and pick out some of his antiques."

My mind goes a zillion miles an hour, churning through the thousands—no, *millions*—of dollars' worth of antiques that man must own. Stuff I'd never dared dream I would touch, let alone own it like he does. "Seriously? I'd love to."

He holds a hand out, and when I accept it, he squeezes my fingers, peering down at me through lashes I'm certain are thicker than my own.

Which makes me realize I should have spent more time on my makeup. And my clothes. And . . . oh geez, my T-shirt says

IF HISTORY REPEATS ITSELF I AM SO GETTING A DINOSAUR. That's . . . embarrassing.

"Thanks. I'm sure you'll do a better job than me. He said something about grabbing the . . . uh . . . fah . . . tool? From his study. And then I knew I was in over my head. What even is that?"

I grin. "This is weird."

"What's weird?"

"You. Not being flawlessly perfect."

"I've never said I was perfect."

I shrug. "I know. You just . . . exude it."

He snorts. "I *exude* perfection."

"Yep. Anyway, he's asking for a chair. Eighteenth century. Carved armrests, upholstered seat and back."

"Oh. Why didn't he just say that?"

I elbow him as we cross the dock, stepping onto the grass. "I don't know, maybe he thought it would be funny to see what you brought him?"

"I guess he's not aware I have a secret weapon," Malik says, draping his arm over my shoulder.

I'm pretty sure I'm about to melt into the grass and create a Holly-shaped puddle, a dopey smile plastered to my face.

I trip on a rock, apparently too distracted by his arm muscles and delicious lips to focus on where I'm putting my feet. I'm abruptly flying toward the ground, about to get my wish of being a puddle, when Malik manages to catch my arm and I end up swinging around and slamming into his chest.

"Uhhhhh . . ." is all I can manage before coughing, trying to regain my breath after slamming into his rock-hard body.

"You're welcome," he says, chuckling, making the heat rise in my cheeks.

"Thank you."

"Shall I carry you to the car, just to be sure you don't bite the dust before then, or . . ."

I swat at his arm and step back. "I can manage."

"Are you sure? Because I need your intimate knowledge of Fuh-tools to save me, and you're no good to me dead," he says, reaching out and tugging a strand of my hair.

"It's *fauteuil*. You're kind of a smart aleck, you know that?"

His smile widens. "Most girls consider my wittiness to be charming."

"I have no idea why," I joke as we approach the valet stand.

It's not until I look up and see Sam, a thirty-something-year-old valet, that the panic spikes. He's smiling at me. Because he recognizes me.

Obviously, he freaking recognizes me!

"Hey, Holiday," he says. "How's it going?"

"Um," I squeak, my chest tightening. "Good."

Malik holds out his valet ticket to Sam, but as he drops it into Sam's palm, it's like the words finally register. He turns from Sam to stare at me, his brow furrowed, the gleam of mistrust sparking in his eyes.

Sam's oblivious, turning his back to us as he opens the key box and grabs Malik's keys. Without another word, he jogs away with them dangling from his fingertip.

"Holiday?"

"Uh . . ." This is my chance to tell him. I could speak the truth and take responsibility for my lies. But . . . I can't. A guy like him walks away when people lie. I can tell already. I tell him the truth, and he's gone.

And it's a fling. *A fling.* It doesn't matter, in the end, what my name is because we're parting ways at the end of the summer. What he doesn't know will never hurt him.

I smile in a way I hope is a mixture of shyness and embarrassment. "See, I kind of have a reputation around here," I say, turning the idea over and over, trying to decide if there are any ways it could backfire. But I don't really have any better options.

"For?"

"Loving holidays!" I say with forced cheerfulness. "Christmas, New Year's, everything. I love 'em all. I really go all out. With, you know, my outfits, and I help Henrietta, uh, decorate the hall."

But as the words leave my mouth, I realize that the Fourth of July is next week. I'm going to have to put on a ridiculous show for this to work.

"Seriously?" I can't tell if he's intrigued or amused or what, but he seems to be buying it.

"Yeah, so, a lot of people around here call me Holiday. You'll totally see what I mean soon—I mean if you want to help me decorate for Independence Day, you should swing through, uh, tomorrow."

"Really?"

"Yeah, I have tons of decorations."

Shoot. I so do not have any decorations. This is going to get really interesting really fast.

"Huh," he says. "Just when I think I have you all figured out . . ."

"Yep, you know me, just full of surprises!"

And lies, many lies.

I turn away from Malik, crossing my arms, watching as his Audi pulls up under the portico. Sam gets out and tosses the keys toward Malik.

Malik snatches them out of the air, and then we're climbing into his car and snapping our seat belts into place.

It only takes Malik moments to navigate the surface streets, whipping around corners and accelerating like we're in some crazy car chase. We're zipping onto the freeway now, and then barreling across the I-90 bridge over Lake Washington at a speed that makes the water blur into a mass of blue. But Malik looks completely at ease. There's no narrowed eyes, no white knuckles. Instead, he leans back into his seat, occasionally glancing my way.

"How'd you learn to drive like this?" I ask as he takes the first exit onshore, rapidly shifting downward as we approach a light.

He shrugs. "My first car was a Lambo. You can't own a car like that and not figure out how to maximize it."

"What's a Lambo?"

He raises a brow. "Lamborghini?"

"Oh. Right. Sorry." I stare out the window and hope he doesn't notice my embarrassment. "So what happened to it?"

"Wrecked it."

I jerk away from the window and look at him wide-eyed, tightening my grip on the door handle. "You wrecked your last car and you still drive like this?"

He chuckles. "That was over a year ago. Before I moved up here to live with my grandpa," he says. "I'm a better driver now."

Before I can ask another question, we're pulling up at a set of fancy swirly iron gates. I had no idea Charles's old place was barely ten minutes away. Okay, fifteen, if a normal person were driving.

I wonder if that's how Malik's mom convinced him to move—telling him it was so close.

Malik pauses, and then the gates are swinging inward, and I don't know if it somehow recognizes his car or someone's watching us on a security screen.

I lean forward, looking upward out the windshield. It's hard to catch my breath as I take in the sprawling mansion. Unlike Cartwell's homage to glass and concrete, this place is . . . traditional.

And this time, I can't keep myself from openly gawking as I get out of the car. It looks like a gothic castle. Like something that belongs on a hillside in 1800s England. There are windows everywhere, trimmed in stonework, set against the brick of the home. Spires jut into the skyline at each corner of the roof.

"I know," he says, his voice level, betraying neither pride nor embarrassment. "It's a lot to take in."

"Mm-hmm," I say, regaining my composure, remembering he thinks I'm related to Henrietta, that I come from money too, even if it's not quite this much.

"If my grandpa ends up liking Sunrise House, we'll have to put it on the market. It's too much for just me. I don't even think I've stepped foot in half the rooms since I moved here a year ago."

I stare up at the house, taking in its grandeur. "I mean, let's get real, you could put an entire orphanage in there and have room left over."

He laughs. "I know."

"So you live here alone?" I ask, following him toward a ridiculously ornamental carriage entrance. I can't help but wonder if this place dates back to the time this overhang actually *was* used for carriages. "Your mom didn't move up here?"

He pauses on the front stoop. "No, she's still in California. She developed a real estate branch of Buchannan Industries before I was born, and she established the headquarters down there."

"Oh."

The front entry is an enormous timber door that could accommodate driving a car inside. It features the same family-crest brass knocker as the one on Charles Buchannan's suite door, except this one is the size of my head.

Malik pushes the door open and steps inside, and I trail after him.

"So, this is where I live," he states simply, as my eyes adjust to the room in front of me. "The bedrooms are all upstairs, but he doesn't need any more bedroom furniture."

There's something a little different about Malik, now that we're here. Something a little more grounded, serious.

Which is totally weird, because people are supposed to be most at ease when they're home. But instead of cracking a joke, tossing his arm around me like he did back at Sunrise House, he just leads me deeper into the cavernous house.

"That grand staircase is . . . ," I say, my voice trailing off. I don't even know what to say about it. It's glorious.

"It's made of hand-carved teak," Malik says, moving away from the entry and toward a hallway. "The spindles were imported from England, from a three-hundred-year-old home that was being torn down, and then they were incorporated into this house when it was built. Some of the stonework is from that same house, actually. My grandfather has a love of English country homes, so that's where the style comes from."

Malik's voice is nearly echoing around in the place as he leads me away from the entryway. "This corridor is modeled after one in the House of Commons. Especially the pillars—"

"Marble," I say, my fingers trailing over the first one. "Your grandpa must be right at home at Sunrise."

He smiles. "Yeah, I may have joked about that the first time I saw them."

"They look better here," I say. "I can't stop thinking that Sunrise House reminds me of some opulent Vegas casino. Too over-the-top, you know?"

He stops in the hall, pivoting on his heel to face me. "I've thought that since the day I walked in."

"Really?"

"Yes," he says, stepping closer. "See, I've grown a little tired of all this."

My mouth grows dry as he makes one last step; scarcely an inch separates us. "Maybe that's what draws me to you."

He's drawn to me. My chest tightens, and it's hard to breathe. There's something in his look, in the wicked curl of his lips.

"Um, what?" I manage to say, and it comes out on a breath.

"There's something . . . *real* about you," he says. "Even when you're surrounded by a failed attempt at old-world elegance."

"Oh," I say, because I can't think, can't move as he leans forward, his eyes darkening.

His lips brush against mine in the barest of kisses, so feather soft that when he pulls away, I'm almost afraid I dreamed it.

And then he steps away, his gaze directed back at the house, and it's almost like it didn't happen. "So, let me give you the *real* tour, shall I?"

"Uh, yeah," I say, reeling.

Malik kissed me. I want to do that stupid thing girls do in movies, touch my fingers to my lips, but I resist.

"Race you to the end," he says, and then abruptly, bursts into a sprint.

I scramble after him, but he has a head start, and it's all I can do to catch up. Doors and columns and coffered ceilings and chandeliers all stream by in a blur as I careen around a corner. I bounce off a wall and can't help the burst of laughter.

This is surreal. I'm racing Malik down the halls of the biggest house I've ever been in, and I can't decipher his odd mood swings. Serious when we arrived, then playful as he kisses me, and now we're racing?

Two enormous, fogged glass doors are up ahead, and I skid to a stop beside him.

"Welcome to the orangery," he says, opening the doors.

As we step inside, it's like I've entered another world. A humid jungle, with such vibrant green foliage that I'm on sensory overload. I almost expect there to be monkeys or parrots or something. It's big enough for it—it's almost as large as a basketball court.

"Wow," I say, my breath escaping me. "This . . ."

I trail off as I look up. The glass walls arch into a series of domes, and in every corner, flower baskets hang with bright purple flowers and vivid green vines trailing toward the floor. Palm trees and orange trees soar upward. Ahead, a walkway curves around a lawn so perfect, so uniformly green, it looks artificial. The edges of the walk are trimmed in flowers—bright blues and reds. The path rises into a bridge that spans a bubbling stream.

"I don't know what to say."

"I want to tell you something," he says, motioning toward an ornate iron bench.

I follow him over and we get situated, him with one foot propped up on his knee as he turns to me. "I spent last summer in Nepal."

"Oh." *Huh?* What's an orangery got to do with Nepal?

"It was after the car wreck. My grandfather felt I should 'repair my image,'" he says, making air quotes. "All the news outlets were speculating on if I'd been drinking and driving, and they were running pictures from parties I'd been to, portraying me as a reckless party boy."

"Were you?" I ask.

"I was sober when I wrecked, but I was on my way to a party, so who knows? I might've driven afterward. Not drunk. Buzzed maybe." He frowns, as if he hasn't realized the truth until this very moment. "The worst part was, the wreck didn't really faze me. The next day I was texting with my friends about going out again. I wasn't going to change."

He chews on his bottom lip, the first nervous tick I've ever seen him do. It's like a chink in his otherwise perfect armor. "But see, my grandfather went into spin control. He didn't like the way my actions reflected on him and Buchannan Industries.

They created a plan to make me look like some sort of do-gooder. My mom was on his side, and they threatened to cut me off if I refused to go."

He's playing with his watch, staring downward as he twists it around and around his wrist. "They set me up with an organization doing relief work for three months. I don't even know why they allowed me to join them, given my reputation. I figure he paid them or funded the whole trip or something. I went there angry and determined to make it through the summer so I could go back to my life and pick up where I left off. I wanted to hang out with my friends. I had premieres to go to and I was dating someone. . . ."

I take in a sharp breath and hope he doesn't notice. "And?"

He looks up at me now, and there's such sincerity in his eyes, it's like I can feel it tug at my heart.

"To say it was a rude awakening would be an understatement." He looks back at his watch again, this time swirling his fingertip against the glass, counterclockwise like maybe he can turn back time. "I hated every minute of it, because for the first time, I didn't have a way to just *check out* from all responsibility. When I didn't want to face reality, I couldn't go back to my big bedroom. I couldn't climb in my fancy car and head to a party. I couldn't jump on our jet and go somewhere else. It was just unrelenting every minute of every day."

"What was so bad about it?"

I don't want to admit it, but I know nothing of Nepal.

"I'm sure there are better parts of the country, but where we were working . . . it was filthy. It smelled, and people were begging on every corner. . . ." His voice trails off, and he rakes in a deep breath, looking up again. "There were homeless children. Everywhere. I couldn't turn around without seeing them. I'd practically trip on them if I wasn't looking."

His eyes bore into mine. "The first time I looked a little girl in the eyes and saw her pain and hunger and despair . . ."

He trails off again and abruptly stands, walking a few feet away and raising his arms, motioning to the orangery around us. "This is what I thought was normal. This is how I lived for eighteen years. And in that one instant, I hated it all. I felt stupid and selfish and like I'd been a complete and utter fool."

"You can't help that you grew up like this."

"Maybe that's true, but I'm *grown* now, and I should be out there helping people. Fixing things."

I stand, stepping into the grass, stopping when we're toe-to-toe. "So do something about it."

"That's just it. I don't know what I'm supposed to do. After I returned, I moved up here and took my place at Buchannan Industries like my grandpa wanted me to. I figured if I straightened out my act, I could develop a plan. I donate my salary and I volunteer as much as possible and it's just . . . it's not enough. I want to change the world, and it's impossible."

I rest my arms on his shoulders, so we're in a loose hug, and stare into his eyes. "So we'll figure it out. Bill Gates doesn't even run Microsoft anymore. He spends all his time on his foundation. You could start one."

"And do what? Every problem I've ever had could be solved by throwing money at it. But this is bigger than that."

"I don't know yet. But we'll think of something."

He reaches forward, tangling his fingers in my hair, his thumb brushing against my cheek. "You're going to be good for me," he says, his voice low and throaty.

And then he kisses me.

Unlike the last kiss, this one is longer than a single heartbeat. I almost believe Malik can turn back time—or at least pause it—because I lose myself in the moment. My eyes shut and the fragrant scent of the flowers mingles with the taste of Malik's lips.

When we finally part, he squeezes my hand, and the world comes back into focus. "So, I guess we should go find the antiques we're supposed to be looking for, huh?"

He leads me out of the orangery and back into the much cooler air of the hall. He clears his throat, and I can feel the awkwardness in the air, like he's not sure how to transition from such intensity. "Um, I've got a short list of specific items, and then we'll just wander the house and see what else we might find to fill his new place."

I follow him down the hall, passing the rooms we'd raced by earlier.

"The study is this way."

I feel like I've gone back in time as we pass a full suit of armor inside a glass case and walk under a series of crystal and plaster chandeliers.

"This place has a ballroom, doesn't it?" I ask.

"It does," he says. "It's in the other wing. I haven't been in it since . . . hmmm . . . I was sixteen."

"You had a sweet sixteen in a ballroom?"

"God, no. It was a Buchannan Industries event. I was required to make an appearance. That's my grandfather's version of charity work. Throw a ball, charge a thousand dollars per guest, and then write a check to someone else's organization so they can do the work. But that's not enough for me. I want to be *part* of it. I want to spend my time, not just my money."

He stops before a set of doors, then pushes them inward.

Mr. Buchannan's study is the most beautiful thing I've ever seen. The walls are covered, floor to ceiling, in shelves with leather-bound books filling every last shelf. One side of the room has a massive fireplace, the hearth tall enough that I think I could walk into it upright. A wingback chair sits next to it.

He points across the room, to where a desk stately enough for the oval office sits, a leather chair behind it, and a second, different chair facing it on the opposite side. "So, I'm guessing that's our . . . um . . ."

"Fauteuil?" I ask, walking across the room, my fingers trailing along the carved wooden back of the chair. Even though I should've known better, some part of me expected a reproduction. This looks like it could've come directly out of 1700s France. The cushioned back and seat are crushed velvet so soft, I half expect it to fall apart as I touch it.

"You really love furniture," he says, watching me.

I glance up, my cheeks warming. "Yeah. You could say that. Stuff like this has lasted so long, it should be loved and taken care of. . . ." I clear my throat. "There's a reason my first class at WSU this fall is art history."

As Malik studies me intently, I give in to my urge to gently press my fingers against the crushed velvet of the chair. "That's, um, the chair he's after. What else have you got?"

"I know where the sideboard is that he wants, but he also said 'and stuff for display.' Like to go on the sideboard and the mantel, and his coffee table . . . and I don't know what he might want. I thought we could bring back the small stuff and then just note the location of the others for one of his assistants to pick up."

I follow him out of the study and down the hall, studying the perfectly tailored way his button-down hugs his shoulders. The sleeves are rolled up, showing just enough skin to make my mouth water.

We round a corner, and then the hallway opens up into a cavernous space.

"Wow . . ." I swallow, staring at the biggest hearth I've ever seen, with a huge, carved mantel above it. "I could stand inside that fireplace."

"Yeah. I've never seen it in use, but it still looks pretty cool."

"That's an understatement."

I step farther into the room, taking in the huge pool table with carved claw-foot legs. In front of it, two sofas face each other, a low coffee table between them, holding a crystal decanter and two snifters.

Malik flashes me a brilliant smile. "I was hoping you could help me move that couch."

I smack his shoulder. "You're such a smart aleck."

I'm drawn toward a table in the corner of the room, where the light from an adjacent window reflects off the jewels of . . . whatever it is . . . some kind of fancy jewelry box. I walk closer, fascinated. "The enameling . . . it reminds me of a Fabergé egg."

"That's because it *is* Fabergé. I mean, not an egg, obviously, but it is made by Fabergé."

I raise a brow. "I've never seen one in real life before."

"I used to love them. Now they just remind me of excess." He frowns. "I guess I like the idea of the surprise, though, inside the egg."

I step away from the Fabergé jewelry box, walking around the room, my hands tracing over the pool table. "Yeah? You like surprises?"

"I like you," he says.

I raise a brow. "What's that got to do with surprises?"

"That's what you are. A refreshing surprise."

Yeah, I'm a surprise all right. As in, *Surprise! My name's not Lucy and I'm not rich!*

"What about that?" I ask, pointing to a brass mantel clock. "It would look good on a dresser or even a side table."

"You think?"

"Yeah, definitely."

"It doesn't really match what he has so far."

"You don't want to be too matchy-matchy. Sometimes an eclectic piece is better. And all the gold tones he's got in the apartment will go with the brass, but the gothic style will make it stand out."

I realize he's staring and grinning. "What are you going to do with all that knowledge you've got crammed up there?" he asks, motioning to my head.

"I want to be a curator. I want to spend my life finding lost pieces of significance, and then making sure people *get* why they're so important to keep. It's easy to lose pieces of our history, you know. People toss stuff in the trash, and they have no idea it's important. If something has lasted two hundred years, it should last two hundred more."

"Well, then, maybe *you* should give *me* a tour of this house. Pretend I've never been here, and you want me to see the significance in all this . . . *stuff.* And then maybe, for once, I won't view it as a giant pile of spent money."

I grin. "I'm in." I point to a pair of candlesticks. "Those, for instance, are in the style of Louis the Sixteenth. They'd be from the late 1700s, if they're real. Part of the style was influenced by all the excitement around the excavation of Pompeii."

I glance over at him to find he's studying the candlesticks with interest. "He was married to Marie Antoinette, you know. Maybe you've heard of her?"

He laughs. "Once or twice."

I lead him over to the fireplace, staring at the portrait hanging over the mantel. "This is baroque."

"I hate it."

"I figured you would. The baroque period was known for its *excess.*" I glance over at him. "How do you live in this house . . . and drive that car . . . if you hate it so much?"

He steps up beside me, so we're shoulder to shoulder, and stares upward at the painting.

"The car is just one of many in the garage. It's not like I went and bought it. And the house . . . It would be a bigger waste to pay rent somewhere else and let it sit empty, I guess."

"Makes sense," I say.

"Does it?" he asks.

"Yeah."

"I'm not so sure," he says, stepping closer, letting his hand trail down my arm. "Lately I think the only thing in my life that makes sense is you."

CHAPTER EIGHT

Three hours later, Malik and I are at Mr. Buchannan's front door. I'm walking slowly, holding the brass mantel clock, paranoid Malik will say something flirty and I'll get flustered and drop it. Malik has the candlesticks, and he tucks one under his elbow so he can unlock and hold open the door for me.

Like he's not at all worried about dropping such priceless antiques.

"Grandpa?" he calls out.

"In here," comes the muffled reply.

We set the items down on the granite counter in the kitchen, and I follow Malik down the hall, to where an open door lets in a slant of light.

"We brought back a few things for you," he says.

"We?"

I step into the room just as he speaks. He glances up, his surprise evident, before his scowl takes over. He's sitting behind a mahogany Victorian-style pedestal desk, a shut laptop in front of him.

With his brow furrowed and his lips turned down, he looks so much older. "I don't want guests."

"Oh," I say, taking a step back. I really shouldn't be here, anyway, since I'm supposed to stay away from him. "I'm sorry, I'll—"

"She helped me pick out a few things at the house," Malik says, reaching for my hand to stop me. "I don't know a thing about your antiques."

"And?" Mr. Buchannan says, crossing his arms.

"And she—"

"Not her. I don't care about her," he says, propping his elbows on his desk and leaning forward with an intense gaze. "I meant, what did you bring me?" he says, his tone still biting. It's hard to believe this is the same man who had so gleefully dragged us to Cartwell's house. He's reverted to the grumpy, caustic man I first met, when he wanted me out of his place.

I want to leave, but Malik is still grasping my hand.

"A clock. And some candlesticks," he offers.

"I pulled together a list of some of the larger items I thought you could use," I say, pulling it out of my back pocket. "Malik arranged for them to arrive tomorrow."

I pull my hand free of Malik's, stepping farther into the room and wondering if it's actually a lion's den. He stares at the paper for a long, silent moment.

"I've lost my glasses," he finally mumbles.

"Oh," I say. "I could read you—"

"I can *read* just fine, I'm not an idiot. I simply need my glasses."

He doesn't look up as he speaks, just keeps staring at the page.

"Um, right," I say, feeling horribly awkward. Does he want help? Does he not want help? I glance over at Malik, pleading for assistance.

"We'll look. Where can you last remember having them?"

"My bedroom. Or in here. I don't know."

His shoulders slump and his voice drops, becoming almost a defeated mumble. I suddenly realize this is a portrait of him I was never meant to see. "I can't remember a dang thing anymore."

Watching this powerful man be reduced to this causes a lump to rise in my throat.

"I'll help you look in here," I say. "Malik can check your bedroom."

"Yes, I'm sure they'll turn up." Malik disappears then, leaving me and Mr. Buchannan alone together.

I turn to the long table spanning one wall, lifting papers and peering into open boxes. When I feel the weight of his gaze, I glance over my shoulder to find him watching me.

Studying me.

"You're not his usual type," he says.

"Uh," I say, not sure how to respond. I picture Selena and Emma and their megawatt smiles, their sparkling dresses. "No, I guess not."

I pick up a newspaper that's been spread out on the table, folding it carefully, hoping to find the glasses underneath. But it's just the table and a paperweight.

"What is it you're after?"

I swallow, glancing back at him. "Excuse me?"

"Why are you pursuing my grandson?"

I furrow my brow. "I mean, I'm not . . . really . . ." I clear my throat. "*Pursuing* him. It's more the other way around, I guess."

He leans back in his chair, crossing his arms and staring me down. I know he's supposedly half-blind without his glasses, but right now, it feels like he's trying to peer into my soul. "Can he trust you?"

"What?"

"Can. He. Trust. You." He repeats, drawing out each word as if I'm stupid.

Wow. Is he worried I'm going to break Malik's heart? Or that I'm using him for his money? "I'm not planning to rob him or screw him over or something. I *like* him. We're having fun."

"He's a fragile boy."

I make a funny choking noise. "I hardly see him that way."

"He's not like me. He has so much to learn to take up where I left off, and he's not ready."

I swallow. "With all due respect, sir, I don't think he *wants* to be exactly like you."

"Nonsense. He's a Buchannan. Everything I built could be his if he'd put in a little effort, but he doesn't have the drive." Frustration leaks through his stoic demeanor, and he throws his hands about as he speaks. "His mother gave him too much freedom, and he spent all his time running around with his little friends in the Hollywood Hills. Now he doesn't know what hard work is."

And that's it. I can't fake being polite anymore. My jaw drops, and indignation sets in. "You think he's *lazy*? You think *that's* why he's not taking over your company at nineteen? Maybe he doesn't *want* to be you. Maybe it has nothing to do with hard work."

"He's exactly like me. He doesn't want to take the company because he didn't build it. He wants to create something of his own. His mother did, too, and I supported the real estate branch she wanted to create. But because of that, the mantle has fallen to him, and he *will* take over my position."

I lean on the table and cross my arms. "Have you even bothered asking *why* he's not driven to become the next Buchannan Industries CEO?"

He narrows his eyes.

"He's destined for big things; you just don't see it. Because you're too busy trying to see him as something else."

"Found them," Malik says, behind me.

I startle, and my cheeks burn, wondering how much of our conversation Malik heard.

Mr. Buchannan holds out a hand, and Malik deposits the glasses in his palm. He puts them on, pushing them up his nose as he picks up the list I've created, as if the whole conversation we had never existed.

The room falls silent as he holds the list up to the light, his eyes roaming the page. I get the sudden feeling I'm a student watching her teacher grade a test.

When he's done reading, he folds the list in half, sets it on his desk, and then looks up at me.

"Good," he says. "You can go now."

"Um, okay," I say, stepping away, unsure if that was a stamp of approval or an annoyed dismissal. "Uh, it was nice to see you again."

Moments later I'm standing in the entry and Malik is giving me an apologetic look. "Sorry," he whispers. "He's not one for guests."

"I noticed."

"It seemed like he liked you, after the whole Goya excursion. But he's been like this since he retired."

"What? Grumpy?"

He sighs, pinching the bridge of his nose. "Yeah. The truth is, he . . . was forced into retirement. The board voted him out."

"Of his own company? They can do that?"

He nods. "Yeah. A few key members didn't always agree with his decisions, and as soon as he got a little forgetful, they used that to force him out. He didn't take it well. He's been angry and bitter for a while."

"And that's why he's so keen on you getting into his business, isn't it?" I say as the truth finally dawns. "He wants you to be there because he can't be."

"Yeah. I guess I'm the next best thing. So I do what he asks, and I go to the office every day and put in the time. But my heart's not in it. And he knows it."

"And does his . . . forgetfulness have anything to do with why he never goes out?"

Malik looks up at the ceiling, as if struggling with the truth of his grandfather's disposition. "He's bitter and angry about being forced out, but I think he's also embarrassed that his mind is slipping. He's afraid to make a mistake in front of anyone.

He's used to being one of the most brilliant men in the entire country. The idea that he's somewhat . . . *mortal* . . . well, he's struggling with it."

He finally looks me in the eyes again. "That's probably why he was annoyed you were here when he was missing his glasses. You saw him in a weak moment."

"Ah," I say, remembering his over-the-top frustration.

So Mr. Buchannan doesn't like to display flaws. It almost makes his gruff behavior forgivable.

"Anyway, I told him earlier that I'd help him unpack some of his books, since he wouldn't trust the movers with them. I'll walk you to your car."

"Oh, um, no, that's okay. I'm going to stop by my grandma's on my way out," I say, reaching for the door.

"Okay. Text me later?"

"Sure."

I think he might kiss me; I want another kiss, but instead, he just gives my hand a little squeeze and then steps away.

Maybe three kisses in one day is too much to ask.

I leave his apartment and head in the direction of Henrietta's door. I glance back, just to be sure he's not watching, and then cruise right past it and head for the elevators.

It's only when those doors slide shut that I finally do it.

I touch my fingers to my lips, remembering how it felt to kiss him in the heat of the orangery.

CHAPTER NINE

The next morning, I'm sitting at a table in Starbucks, a mile from Sunrise House, when Alex breezes in with Rena in tow.

My heart does this weird, painful spasm as they laugh, approaching the front counter, oblivious to me sitting at a tiny table next to the fireplace.

Alex said she had to help her mom with some project today, that she was too busy to come over and hang out. My eyes trail over the bundle of shopping bags in Rena's hand. Forever 21. Macy's. Abercrombie.

They've been shopping all day. Alex doesn't even *like* shopping, but apparently she's willing to schlep from store to store with Rena?

I glance at the side door, considering whether I should just get up and slink out. But before I can move, Rena flicks a glance over her shoulder, and then she does a double take, her pale pink lips turning into a tiny O as she stares at me.

She knows. She totally knows that Alex blew me off, which means they talked about me, and about how Alex wanted to ditch me for some reason . . . ugh.

My heart feels heavy in my chest as I force my lips to curl into an easy smile and lean back into the leather easy chair, watching as Rena elbows Alex, and Alex turns around to see me.

Alex plays her part better, smiling like she's surprised in a good way, like she's pleased about running into me as she waves. She says something to Rena—handing her some cash—and heads in my direction.

I go to cross my legs, so that I can appear *oh so casual*, but the table in front of me is low, and I end up kicking over my coffee cup.

The cup tumbles over and the lid busts open, the coffee sloshing across the little wicker table, soaking into every crevice. I jerk upright and dab at the wicker with the tiny square napkin I'd received with my coffee. Alex veers off her course to grab a handful of napkins, and then we're both dabbing at the table and not speaking and my cheeks feel too warm and I'm annoyed and . . .

"That sucks," Alex finally says, tossing the sopping napkins into a nearby garbage can. "Want me to order you another one?"

"Sure you have time for that?" I ask, unable to keep the bite from my tone.

If she's surprised that I called her out, she's not showing it. "Yeah, my mom wasn't feeling well, so we decided to save mulching the garden for another day. I would've called you, but then Rena texted and I got side-tracked."

"Oh," I say, not sure I buy it.

"Do you want to go get manicures with us?" she asks, tossing my empty cup into a nearby trash can. "I'm sure they can squeeze you in. Our appointment is in ten minutes."

Appointment? Had they made it in advance or only just this morning?

"Nah," I say, standing. "I gotta go back home. Figured I could work a couple more hours. I only have, like, six weeks left to save for school."

"Oh. Okay." She stands there awkwardly, glancing back at Rena. I can see she wants to go, but instead, her feet remain planted on the floor in front of me. "Have you run into Malik again yet?"

I can't help the grin that overtakes me. Immediately, Alex smiles back, and I can practically *see* her shoulders sink in relief that we're talking about something else. "Um, yeah."

"So? Dish!"

"He brought me to his house."

Her jaw drops. "The castle-looking mansion on the lake?"

I nod.

"Dang! I've seen pictures of the outside online. What's it like?"

"It's crazy," I say. "I lost track of the number of rooms, and we didn't even make it off the ground floor."

"And?" she says, moving her hand in a come-on, out-with-it gesture.

"And he has a lot of antiques?"

"I meant, and what were you doing there? Did he invite you over for dinner? Oh," she asks, her face lighting up, "did he cook for you?"

"No, nothing like that. It wasn't a date or anything. We were just grabbing some stuff for his grandpa. The whole thing was an hour, tops."

For some reason, I just can't bring myself to tell her the *other* side I saw of Malik. The gentle, inspired, yet somehow unsure side of him. The one who questions who he is and who he wants to become.

No, Alex wants to know about the boy everyone else reads about. The one on Google.

She grins in an I'm-not-buying-that-you-didn't-make-out-with-him sort of way, but she doesn't press. "And is he still flirting with you?"

"You could say that."

"Seriously, you are a really bad storyteller," she says, crossing her arms. "I need details."

"We kissed."

She gasps. "Like on the cheek?"

I shake my head. "Um, no, like, for real."

She squeals enthusiastically, and it reminds me of a golden retriever. "I can't even believe you're dating *Malik Buchannan*. Everyone we know is going to be so jealous."

I pause. "Wait, *what*? You can't tell anyone about this!"

"Why not?"

"Um, because he thinks I'm someone else? The less people who know about him, or us, or whatever, the better. We're not even dating. It's very casual."

"Well, it's not like you're going to let him slip through your fingers, right?"

"Um, I guess?" Judging by her expression, I think she wants to throttle me. Like Malik is the giant, juicy fish, and I am stupid for not acting like I'd do anything to ensure he doesn't get away. "Anyway, I have plans, so I'm going to get going," I say, standing. I can't analyze things with Malik yet. I can obsess over him in private, but talking about him makes it seem like I think it's a real, lasting thing, and I can't think like that, not when everything we have is built on such a shaky foundation.

"Okay," she says. "See you around?"

I grab my purse, slipping the strap over my shoulder. "Yeah. Text me later."

"Okay. Bye."

She heads back to where Rena is waiting for their drinks, and I slip out the side door, ignoring the weight in my chest as I remember that they have manicure *appointments*. How could they both have appointments if she was supposed to help her mom all day? She only likes going to a specific nail place, and it's always booked up, like, three days out.

Alex has never lied to me. She wouldn't start now.

Would she?

CHAPTER TEN

On July first, with only a few days to spare, I remember my *I love holidays* lie. So I'm sitting cross-legged in the hall outside Henrietta's apartment, leaning over a strip of blue paper.

I curl it into a loop, slipping it around a red circle, and then grab the glue stick on the ground next to me, swiping it on the end of the paper before pinching it together.

Two down, one bajillion to go.

I hold it between my thumb and pointer finger, picking up my phone again. With one hand, I open a message to Alex, then type You sure you can't stop by? So. Much. Work.

I set my phone down and then pick up another strip, this one red, and repeat the formation of the loop.

My phone chirps and I glance over at it. I don't have to unlock the screen again to see Sorry. Busy.

I roll my eyes, reaching for the glue stick. If it takes thirty seconds per ring and I want to make a chain for each side of the hall, and it has to be, oh, fifty feet long, that's . . .

That's too much math, is what it is. There's a reason I prefer history.

"Channeling your inner kindergartener?" calls a familiar voice.

I look up to see Malik striding toward me, grinning.

"It's starting to feel that way," I say. "I'm a little late on the holiday decorations this year. And I may have underestimated just how large this hallway is."

"And you weren't able to find anyone to force into slave labor, either," he says.

"Nope."

Before I can protest, he's sitting down next to me, leaning back against the wall as he picks up a pair of scissors.

"You don't have to help me," I say.

"You're doing me a favor. I'm supposed to go back to the office this evening to finish up a project, and I'm procrastinating."

"Yeah?"

"Yeah. Each month, I'm going through a crash course of different departments in the company, and this one is advertising. I have huge e-mail chains to read through, and binders full of old ads, and . . ." He sighs, like he's overwhelmed or bored at the mere idea.

"Sounds delightful."

"You can see why I would rather play with glue sticks."

"Then, by all means," I say, motioning to the art supplies I have strewn about.

I know it's risky to sit out here in the hall like this, next to Malik, but there are only four penthouse suites on this wing. Three, if you don't count Henrietta. And the two residents at this end of the hall—Byron and Ruth—happen to be besties and are away on a Caribbean cruise. So I figure it's a pretty safe place to sit without anyone blowing my cover.

"Let's make a deal. I'll help you make enough to cover this hall, and then we do an extra strand for my office. It's really quite stuffy. It could use . . ."

"More shoddy art?"

"I'm tired of how serious that place is. And I wouldn't mind something to remind me of you whenever I'm sitting at my desk."

I smile, meeting his eyes. "Okay, then, deal."

I push a stack of red and blue paper toward him and pick up a few of the strips I already cut. He grabs a white strip, twisting it so the two ends meet.

"So . . . ," I say, wracking my head for a conversation starter. "Um, where's your favorite place in the world?"

"This hallway is right up there," he says, reaching for the glue stick.

"I'm serious," I say, hoping I don't blush at his comment. He is entirely too good at flirting or complimenting or whatever. I try not to think of how much practice he's probably had.

"Why?"

"It's this thing my grandma does. She asks everyone about their favorite place."

"Oh."

"Yeah. So what's yours?"

"Um," he says, staring up at the ceiling for a second. "I guess I don't have one."

"Oh, come on. You've probably traveled all over the world. You've *got* to have a favorite place."

"Can I get back to you on that?"

"I guess." I hold out my growing chain, letting him slip a new loop onto the end.

"What about you?" he asks.

"I'll show you sometime. After you tell me yours."

"I'm going to hold you to it," he says, picking up a scrap of red paper.

I lay out my little chain of four on the floor. "How long do you think this is going to take us?"

"Hopefully forever." He grins. "But most likely . . . a couple of hours."

"Yeah. You're probably right. It'll just *feel* like forever."

"Let's make a deal," he says. "Whoever puts together enough to span the hall first, wins."

"Wins what?"

"The choice of where we go on our next date."

"Deal."

Malik has an assigned parking stall, right next to the front entry of Buchannan Industries' building C. This fact should not surprise me, but I keep looking at the metal sign, at where it says RESERVED FOR MALIK BUCHANNAN in big block letters. I've started to think of him as simply *Malik*, the person and not the icon, but that sign puts it all back in my head.

I climb out of his car, staring upward at his office tower. It's the tallest building on campus, all sparkling, black-tinted glass.

"Twenty-one floors," he says, from where he's standing on the sidewalk. He's got a twelve-foot-long, red-white-and-blue chain gathered in his hands.

"Oh. Must have a nice view of the lake," I say as I step up onto the curb.

"It does." He leads me down the walkway, and then we turn and step under the shade of a big frosted awning. There's one of those revolving doors, and Malik lets me push through first.

Inside, we're greeted by a cold blast of AC. And silence.

Complete silence.

A guard sits behind a wide, glossy black desk. "Evening, Mr. Buchannan," he calls as we pass by. Malik nods in response but doesn't speak.

There are four elevators on either side of us, and when he hits the up key, one immediately dings.

I step inside, turning to hit the 21 button.

Malik raises a brow. "How did you know?"

The doors slide shut. "Please. Like they're going to put you on, say, the second floor with accounting."

He smirks. "Accounting is on the third floor. Second is IT."

"Right," I say, playfully patting him on the back. "So my point stands."

The doors open on the twenty-first floor, and we step out of the elevator, where an enormous curved desk sits. A big BUCHANNAN INDUSTRIES logo hangs over it, the words EXECUTIVE OFFICE below.

But the chair is empty, and most of the overhead lights are off. Probably because it's seven thirty. Malik was wrong when he guessed a couple of hours to make those chains. It took us four. But I don't think he has any doubt of my dedication to holidays now.

We pass door after door, each of them with big placards that have words like CEO and VICE PRESIDENT.

We stop at the end of the hall, in front of a dark, cherry-wood door. The placard simply reads, MALIK BUCHANNAN.

I point at the brass placard, giving him a quizzical look. "What, no title?"

He keys in a code to the button on the door, not meeting my eyes. It's almost like he's *embarrassed* that his name is all that matters, not a title. "No. I'm still getting to know the way the company works, so I don't have an official role here yet. I can't lead a company I don't know."

He pushes the door open, and my eyes widen.

I'm facing a wall that is nothing but windows, from floor to ceiling, wall to wall. Lake Washington stretches out below us, but it's the opposite of the view at Sunrise House. I can see Mercer Island. To the right, cars zip across the bridge, looking like little ants marching in a row. The lake is inky blue, sprinkled with sailboats.

"This was my grandfather's office," Malik says.

"They let him keep it? Or give it to you, I guess?"

He shrugs. "Some of the board members didn't like how he was treated. They didn't feel it was right for anyone but a Buchannan to sit at this desk."

I walk over, pulling out his chair and plopping down behind his work space. "So this is what you do all day?"

"Most days. My 'tutorial' of the company is almost over, and then I need to pick something to focus on. My grandfather wants to expand into some new products. Textiles, maybe home-improvement stuff. I'm considering focusing on that. Maybe if we had fulfillment centers in new states or I found some businesses that needed a bigger selling platform, it could create jobs or something. I don't know."

"Why did he focus on American-made products?" I ask, glancing around the office and wondering what it looked like when Charles inhabited it. It's so . . . vanilla. It could be a CEO's office at any company in the world. There's nothing to indicate Charles Buchannan has some grandiose love of America.

I mean, I guess I don't know what I expected. A giant tile mosaic of the American flag on the floor?

"His parents—my great grandparents—grew up during the Depression. Mom said they never let go of some of their habits, like how they didn't trust banks, so they'd hide all their cash under their bed or something. Anyway, they were pretty poor when my grandpa was a kid, and apparently a little proud, too, because they wouldn't accept handouts. So he figured out a way to make money on his own."

"The lemonade," I say, remembering a story I'd once read about Charles Buchannan. He said the first American-made product he ever sold was a glass of lemonade, freshly squeezed by his own hands. His parents couldn't force him to refund the money, since the customers had, in fact, traded their coin for a product and therefore it wasn't charity.

"Yeah. He was only twelve. By fifteen, he'd developed a handwritten catalog of products, and he'd go door to door, selling them on behalf of various people who lived in town. Furniture, cleaning products, clothing, you name it. And instead of pitching people on the product, he'd pitch them on who made it—that the overalls were made by that nice lady down the street who is expecting her third child, or that the furniture was hand-carved by a World War II vet. He was so successful that he started drafting his friends to help, and by the time he turned eighteen, the catalog was printed on glossy pages and distributed countywide."

"Pure brilliance," I say.

"Exactly. He stuck with the catalogs for a few decades before opening the online storefront, and it exploded from there."

"Do you think he believes in it? In the mission statement on the Web site, that is. About how the goal of the company is to *help people help themselves*?"

"He does. I don't think he could grow the company like he did if he didn't believe in it."

"It's not such a bad way to spend your life, you know," I say.

He sighs. "I know. But this place . . . it runs just fine without me. I don't *matter* here."

My eyes rove over the blank walls, the perfectly tidy bookshelves, the boring, generic rug. "There's nothing of you in this room."

"I know. I can't bring myself to decorate an office I don't even want to occupy in the first place."

"Yet, you come here every day," I state.

"What would you do if you were me? Pack a bag of supplies and run off to whatever random country looks to be in the worst shape? Write massive checks to charities that already have people on the ground and concrete goals in place? I'm nineteen years old. I don't know what's best."

He sits down on his desk then reaches over, pulling me to my feet and up against him, so that I'm standing between his legs and his arms are wrapped around my waist. He rests his head on my shoulder and grows quiet.

"Why don't you call the group you went to Nepal with? Ask them how they can partner with Buchannan Industries. And if they don't have ideas, then ask another group and another. Just don't give up. Don't just sit in here day after day after day and forget who you want to become."

When he kisses me, this time, it's raw and hungry, and I let him tangle his hands in my hair.

I kiss him until we're both breathless, the sun setting behind us.

CHAPTER ELEVEN

My favorite place in the world, the antiques store Then and Now, is coated in dust. It's the place I didn't tell Malik about when he asked. My theory is that the owner, a surprisingly young guy who sits behind the counter all day reading *The Wall Street Journal* with his glasses perched at the end of his long, crooked nose, feels that the dust makes all the antiques look older than they actually are. He probably buys the dust in bulk and spends each night flinging it around like some twisted fairy godmother, instantly aging all his merchandise.

Judging by the near-constant turnover of products in this place, his ploy is working.

I trail my finger over a blue vase, absently thinking that the gold paint and gem-colored enameling make it looks like a poor man's version of a Fabergé. I swirl my finger along the design, studying the curves of the vase.

This was exactly what I needed to get my mind off of . . . everything. An afternoon of antiquing. I can't really afford to buy anything, at least not without dipping into my college funds, but oh well. It's still fun to look.

There's something vaguely Italian about the vase. I imagine some artist in his tiny studio, the light reflecting off the nearby canals and illuminating his work. He's hunched over the vase, his eyes narrowed, the paintbrush perfectly still in his hand as he leans in and swirls the bristles across the surface to create the dazzling design.

Someday I'll be able to afford treasures like this. I'll research the history of each piece and display them for everyone to see and admire.

"Why am I not surprised?" a voice calls out. I twist around so fast, the vase tumbles from my fingertips. Malik bolts forward, sort of skidding on his knees, miraculously catching it before it shatters at my feet.

I cringe. "Um, thanks? But also not really because you shouldn't be sneaking up on people like that."

"I was not *sneaking*."

"Oh." I accept the vase from his outstretched hand, turning to set it on the display case beside us. "Wait, why are you here? You probably don't even like antique stores. Were you looking for me?"

He grins. "I waved right at you through the front window, but you were lost in thought. I'm on my lunch break and was just heading to grab a bite to eat next door. Then I saw you. You know, standing near the window, in plain view?"

"Ah. Um, I see." My cheeks may just burst into flames at any moment.

"I mean, you *are* cute, and totally stalkable, but I have your number, so none of that is necessary."

I pretend to be super interested in the claw-foot tub on the floor next to us, leaning over to examine the brass fixtures so my hair will swing forward and hide the heat in my cheeks.

"Join me for lunch," he says, and it comes out as more of a command than a request, reminding me of just how used to getting his way he is.

"Oh," I say, standing up abruptly. Right. Why do I still feel so awkward and dorky? We've spent enough time together that I should feel normal. Natural. Not robotic. But that's the power of Malik. "Um, yeah, sure."

"Your enthusiasm is astounding," he says, deadpan.

I can't help it. I laugh, and my nerves fizzle out, and we're picking up where we left off. "Sorry. Yes. Lunch. Let's do it."

Ten minutes later I'm sipping on a lemonade at the café next to the antique store, out on a deck that overlooks the lake. It's still weird to live in this area, with all its expensive homes and yacht clubs.

"That was my favorite place," I say, breaking the silence.

"The antique store?"

"Yeah. Every time I go in there, I find something new. It's like a free museum."

He smiles. "I figured you'd be drawn to a place like that. Kinda looked at home, you know?" He leans back against his chair and stretches his legs out under the table. Our calves touch, but he doesn't move. He just lets his bare skin rest against mine.

It's driving me crazy. In a good way.

"I've decided where mine is," he says.

"Yeah?"

He nods. "It's you."

My heart flutters. "Huh?"

"My place is you."

"But I'm not a place. That doesn't count."

"It does to me. Because you don't look at me in the same way as everyone else. You don't *want* things from me. When I'm with you—wherever we are—I can forget that I'm supposed to be the heir apparent to the Buchannan Empire and just feel like a normal guy."

"Who's everyone?"

"My grandpa. My mom. Freaking *Time* magazine."

I narrow my eyes, wondering if that came up in Alex's search about him. "You were in *Time*?"

He nods. "Yeah. Last year they did this focus on 'the next generation,'" he says, using air quotes. "Sons and daughters of influential people. Apparently, I was poised to expand my grandfather's empire, but my 'troubling lifestyle,'" he says, using the quotes again, "could derail that."

"Troubling lifestyle?"

"Yeah, you know, the old me." He leans in on his elbows, staring directly into my eyes. "You're the first person who actually gets it. I've *told* my old friends, but it doesn't seem to sink in. They grew up like I did. They're used to the expectations, the lifestyle, and they don't seem to register the fact that it's not what I want anymore."

"Do you still talk to them?"

"No. Once I changed, they grew bored of me. They moved on, and I did too. And it finally registered just how superficial my relationships had been. They never cared about me; they just enjoyed the money and the invitations that came with my name."

"Ouch."

"Yeah. It's nice to meet someone who's different. Who I can actually trust to tell me the truth, you know?"

I smile, but I'm sure it appears plastic. He trusts me.

He shouldn't.

CHAPTER TWELVE

Three days later, I'm sitting on my bed, my feet propped up against the wall, staring at a collage of me and Alex. She's got a nearly identical one in her room, filled with the same pictures. There's one of us at the beginning of the fourth grade, our hair in funky curls because we'd decided to get creative with a tiny-barreled curler at her house. The results were far from glamorous. Then there's one of us at the sixth-grade walkathon, waving peace signs at the camera.

Us at homecoming junior year, when we went stag.

Us at prom this year. I went with Hunter Johansson, the only boyfriend I've ever had. Alex and Rena went stag, but we all shared a limo that Alex's parents rented. Hunter Johansson dumped me the next day. I'm pretty sure he lost interest in me the very instant he saw Finley Denton's cleavage in her sparkling red dress.

Alex was there to buy me ice cream and tell me he didn't deserve me. She was there to draw devil horns on him when we got our yearbooks. I don't know that I loved Hunter, but I guess I thought it was going somewhere. He's even going to WSU like me, even if he did pick it because it has a reputation as a party school and not because of any particular academic program.

I stare at Alex's pretty updo, wondering if that was the moment when things went from ice cream and rom-com marathons to ditching me for Rena. Maybe while I was busy dancing with Hunter, they had some great epiphany of all the things they have in common.

I mean, I guess I knew things would change after we graduated. Alex and Rena are both going to UW, and I'm not. This isn't just some regular old summer vacation. At the end of it, we're going to be hundreds of miles apart.

But I still thought—

My door flies open, and I crane my neck around to see Alex waving a copy of *US Weekly* with so much enthusiasm, she may as well be directing traffic.

"Your boyfriend is in here," she says, flinging the magazine at me. It spins through the air, landing open on my bed.

I twist around, hoping she doesn't notice that I've been staring at the collage, and drop my feet to the floor and pick it up. "I already told you, he's not my boyfriend. And where have you been lately, by the way? I texted you, like, three times in the last week and you've ignored me."

"Busy. But anyway, flip to page twenty-two."

Butterflies swarm as I flip through the pages, ultimately landing on a "Stars: They're Just Like Us!" feature.

And there he is, walking down the street with a bulldog at the end of a red leash.

"I didn't know he had a dog," I say, my eyes roving over the bulky white dog. "I wonder where it was when I was at his house. I mean, it's really big."

"That's what you come back with? I didn't know he had a dog?"

"What? I didn't." I slap the magazine shut. "He's never mentioned it. Maybe it's not his."

"Your boyfriend . . ." At my glare, she pauses and sighs. "The guy you went on a date with and are *hanging out with* is in *US Weekly*. As in the magazine on every checkout stand in every grocery store. And you're concerned about whether he has a dog?"

"I know, I know," I say, sighing. "This is crazy."

"What? No. This is totally awesome! How can you not think so?"

"Because this isn't what he wants to be known for. I think."

"Huh?"

"He wants to make a difference in the world, and they're focused on him walking a freaking dog. That's all people think of—that he's cute and he dates movie stars and goes to big parties. But he doesn't want to be in magazines. Not for this, anyway."

Alex whistles and plops down on my bed. "Wow. You're getting in deep."

"I am not," I say. "It's a fling. It has to be. He thinks I'm Lucy."

"Is that what you want?"

"That's what it needs to be," I say, with conviction. "Now that I know him, I realized how much it's going to hurt him if he finds out I'm lying. Everyone who has ever gotten close to him has betrayed him. If he finds out I'm no better, it'll destroy him. When I go away to college, we'll just naturally drift apart, and that will be that."

As the words come out, I realize how true they are.

"You're sure?" Alex looks at me with concern. "I mean, you kind of sound like you're getting in a little deeper than a *fling*."

"I'm sure," I say resolutely. It's the only thing that makes sense. The only *logical* resolution to this whole thing. "It's just a fun summer romance. That's all it's going to be. He won't know I lied, and he can move on with his life and focus on his goals."

"Okay, so you have, like, six weeks to have fun." She gives me a wicked smile, and I laugh for the first time since she's walked into my room.

"Yeah. I guess so."

"So we just need to be sure your lie isn't uncovered, then."

"Right."

Alex lies back on the bed and turns onto her side, tracing her finger over a big violet dot in the pattern of my comforter. "I have an idea."

"Um, why do I have a serious sense of dread right now?"

"My mom has been going nuts buying me all these back-to-school clothes. It's way more than I can fit in a dorm room, and I swear she thinks I'm going to MIT or Wall Street or something. It's very . . ." Her voice trails off. "Fancy. And you know me. I'd rather wear stuff from the Sounders pro shop than the mall. We could give you a makeover with my brand-new, totally unwanted wardrobe. You could dress more like him. Make sure he doesn't pick up on your . . ." Her gaze roams over me. "Differences."

"You don't have to give me your new clothes."

Alex stands, and I know her mind's already made up. "You'll be doing me a favor. As long as my mom doesn't see the clothes hanging in my closet in a few weeks, she'll figure I packed all of it. And then I don't have to take it. I'll put my pillows in boxes or something so she doesn't notice how light I'm packing." She motions up and down her body. "Come on, you know this is me. I wouldn't be caught dead in a plaid skirt."

She's wearing a lime green Sounders FC T-shirt, blue jeans, and pink Converse sneakers. "Just come over. My mom's at work until six. If you don't like the stuff, don't take it. Okay?"

I sigh, climbing up off my bed. "Okay. Let's go. But you have to drive. My car is almost on empty, and I don't want to dip into my college fund."

CHAPTER THIRTEEN

Alex beams at me as she pulls under the portico outside Sunrise House, flipping her wavy blond hair over her shoulder. I'm sitting in the passenger seat, pretty much buried in shopping bags, feeling like she's my fairy godmother. Except instead of a single night, she's done enough to transform me for six weeks. I can't wait to wear this stuff in front of Malik. Alex was right—it's going to help me feel more on his level.

I don't know how I'm going to get all this stuff to fit in my sure-to-be-tiny dorm room closet in a few weeks, but I don't even care.

"You're totally going to give Selena Gomez a run for her money," Alex says as she puts her car in park. "In fact, both of you are short and dark-haired. You should see if she needs a body double."

I snicker, giving Alex a pointed look. "I'm sure her manager will be calling at any moment." I unbuckle my seat belt, reaching into the backseat for the other shopping bags. "I know I already said it, but seriously—thank you. I can't even believe you don't want to keep this stuff for yourself."

"No biggie. You know how my mom is; always hoping I'm going to magically decide to dress girly at any moment. It's never going to be my style. Besides, you'd do the same for me, right?"

We lock eyes, and the urge to say something—to ask her why she's been ditching me lately—swells. Today has been amazing. Like the friendship we've always had, the one I always thought would span decades. Not the one that's been fizzling away since graduation.

Since before graduation, really.

"Whoooooooa, is that what he drives?"

I glance up from the bag I'm gripping to see a familiar silver sports car glide up to the front entry, stopping next to the valet sign.

It's a good thing he's never asked me to drive, or the fact that I park in the *resident* garage would give me away.

And, you know, the flaking paint, the dented fender, and the broken exhaust.

"Um, yeah," I say, the butterflies in my stomach taking flight. "At about ninety miles an hour. It's terrifying."

"I mean, that thing must be like a hundred grand, easy."

My palms feel sweaty, and I wipe them on my skirt, then cringe at the vague blotches on the gray, recycled T-shirt material. Great. Why did I not put one of these outfits on while I was at Alex's house?

When he climbs out of the car, Alex lets out a low whistle. "Wow," she says, "pictures don't do him justice."

He's wearing deep-blue jeans that hug his hips, along with a pink button-down with rolled-up sleeves, and glasses. I didn't know he wore glasses. Then again, maybe he doesn't. They could be for fashion or whatever.

They're dark, chunky frames, and I get a sudden, overwhelming image of him working at the office late at night, bathed in the light of his laptop.

I open my mouth to say something, but before I can, the dome light clicks on and Alex is getting out of the car and walking toward him while I sit, frozen.

I hiss out a low breath and climb out too, trying to straighten my skirt as I dash after her. He catches a glimpse of me when he's halfway to the front doors, and his step falters as his eyes light up. "Lucy," he says, grinning at me.

Lucy. Every time he says it, I want to correct it, just to hear the way my name would sound on his lips.

But no. I'll never hear it. That's not part of the plan.

"Hey, Malik," I say, accepting his hug. "Um, this is my friend Alex. The one I told you about."

Alex beams, extending her hand. "I've heard so much about you."

My face pretty much bursts into flames.

"Oh?"

"Mm-hmm," she says. "I mean, Holl—" She catches herself just as my heart does a double beat. "Lucy told me you were *super* cute, and I was sure a human being could not possibly live up to her descriptions, but hey, you do a pretty good job."

It's all I can do not to elbow her in the ribs.

He smiles, that casual, self-confident smile that looks just as good in person as it does on the red carpet. "Yeah?"

"Yep, we went shopping today, and now I'm just dropping her off . . . you know, to visit her grandma."

And my mom thought *I* was a terrible liar.

He smiles warmly. "That's nice of you. Are you coming in with us?"

"Oh, gosh, no. I'm not into . . ." She swallows. "Um, old people."

I nearly choke on my laughter, darting a glance away so Malik won't catch my amusement.

"I thought I'd just wait for her in the car. Lots of Candy Crush to play, after all," she says, wiggling her phone.

"Oh, you don't have to do that," he says, glancing over at me. "I can drop you off when you're done visiting."

My mouth goes dry. He can't drop me off. I'm already home.

"That's super nice of you to offer," Alex rushes. "But seriously, I have no plans whatsoever today, and I am completely stuck on this level. I don't mind hanging out."

By the tone of her voice, I know she realizes her misstep. She's just laid a trap that we both fell into, and now she's trying to claw her way out of it.

"Don't be silly," Malik says. "I was actually hoping she could come over to my grandfather's place, anyway. He's been asking about her. So it might be a while. You don't have to wait. It's no trouble at all."

Abort. Abort. Abort.

"Um, okay . . . uh . . . if you're sure," she says, flashing me a frantic look. I'm sure if we both had telepathy, our conversation would look something like, *OH NO. WHAT DO I DO? WHAT DO I DO? WHAT DO I DO?* "I mean, we don't want to put you out. . . ."

"Not at all." He flashes her one of his most charming smiles. I'm pretty sure she immediately forgets entirely why she's protesting, because she just smiles blankly back, leaving me to scramble for a way to fix this.

"Uh, great!" I say as my gears finally start to turn again. "Um, I just need to grab something out of her car, and then I'm all set. Meet you at . . . the front door," I say. Which seems super stupid, because we're standing right next to it.

"Sure."

I tug Alex's elbow, dragging her back toward her car, my insides churning.

"Shoot," she whispers, once we're out of ear shot. "Sorry. I should've seen that one coming."

We both climb into her car, slamming the doors so we can talk without having to whisper.

"What am I going to do?" I despair. "Find some random house for him to drop me off at?"

I pretend to dig into the bags in the backseat so that Malik thinks I'm looking for . . . whatever it is. The tissue paper in the first bag crinkles between my fingers.

But I don't miss that he's staring over here, and at any moment he may decide to walk over and find out what I'm doing sitting in her car.

"Wait! I have an idea," Alex says. "Here." She takes her key chain out of her pocket, sliding a silver key off the ring. "As long as he drops you off before six, no one will be at my house.

You can use the key like it's yours. And then just wait in my room and text me, and then I'll come get you and bring you back here."

Instantly, I picture Alex's house, a beautifully restored Craftsman in a million-dollar neighborhood.

It could work.

"But if I have your key, you can't go home. What are you going to do for the next couple of hours?"

"Um, give me *your* key. I'll wait for you guys to go in and then sneak this stuff into your apartment and put it all away. I can watch TV for a little while until you text me. And I'll move my car into the resident garage so Malik doesn't see it out the window or something."

Hesitation sets in. This is all so elaborate. My simple lie isn't supposed to be so . . . *deliberate*. "Are you sure?"

"Of course," she says, a grin taking over. "Just go hang out with him and catalog every single thing he says and does and tell me all about it later. A girl needs details if she's going to live vicariously."

I grin as I shove the key into my pocket. "You're the best."

"I know," she says, leaning across me and popping the door open. "Now go have fun with Prince Charming."

I slide out of the car, clicking the door shut behind me. Alex starts it back up and is gone a moment later, and I'm crossing the aggregate patio, wondering why it is I ever questioned our friendship.

CHAPTER FOURTEEN

My heart climbs into my throat as we step into his grandfather's apartment, bracing myself for some surly remark the moment he sees me. I pause in the entry, listening to the bubbling of the lion's head fountain.

Nothing yet, just the ticking of a clock and the tinkling of the fountain.

"So . . . was he really asking about me?"

"Yeah. Ever since the stuff we picked out arrived."

"Oh." Relief. Maybe he won't bite my head off this time. Maybe he'll actually *welcome* me into this space.

I follow Malik in the living room, then stop when I see Mr. Buchannan.

He's standing at the windows, his back to us as he stares out at the lake, his arms crossed and his shoulders stiff. He's . . . foreboding, like this. It's as if I can actually *see* him lording over his domain, his company.

"Grandpa?"

When he turns, his eyes land on me. I wait for his expression to shift. I wait for him to scowl or frown. Instead, he *almost* smiles, the corners of his lips half lifting.

"Lucy," he says, his voice is even but has a hint of pleasure. Like maybe he might be happy I'm here.

"Yeah, hi." I flash him my warmest, most confident smile, shoving the butterflies down deep. He may be grumpy, but he's not going to bite.

"I don't know what to do with the desk you picked out," he says, almost . . . kind. "I already have one in my office."

"Oh," I say, brightening. Yes. I can handle this conversation. "I mean, it doesn't have to be used as a desk. We can repurpose it. What room is it in?"

"Follow me," he says, stepping away from the window. He reaches for his cane, then limps past me, back down the hall where his office is. He stops at a doorway across from his home office, pointing inside.

It's a surprisingly large space, with an amazing view of the lake. The room is square, probably sixteen feet in each direction, except for where the soaring window is set into the wall, creating an alcove.

I stare. "Um, you could move those chairs," I say, motioning to where two seats face each other along the wall. "You could place them near the window. And put that table between them. That way your guest could enjoy the view."

The words are out before I think about them. Before I realize he never has guests. To avoid his reaction, I turn in the room, taking in the furniture, including the desk that has been sitting on the wall opposite the chairs, puzzling through the options.

I clear my throat, hoping he hasn't picked up my sudden awkwardness. "Instead of using it as a desk, you could stage it as a sideboard. For tea, maybe?" I say, thinking back to the coffee cup that had been sitting on the counter, a discarded tea bag on the saucer. "If you did loose leaf, you could put different varieties of tea in decorative canisters and have everything you need in here. Other than the hot water, obviously. It might not be that practical, but it would look good. And you could have your, uh, guest sit there, by the window, with you. It's more intimate than the living room."

"I don't have guests," he says, but his hand glides over the smooth wood of the desk, as if considering the way it would look as a repurposed sideboard for tea.

"You could," I say. "It's such a shame for this view to go un—"

"No."

I tip my head to the side, studying the thin line of his lips, the set of his shoulders.

He's not as gruff as he first appears. He's . . . guarded.

It seems odd for a man of his accomplishments to care what others think of him, but he does. I realize that he doesn't dislike people at all. He just has a wall up. A *mile-high* wall.

He's not the iron man I thought he was.

"Henrietta likes tea," I offer. "I could invite her over sometime."

Something glimmers in his eyes. He's considering it.

But then he just says, "No, but I like your idea for the desk. It'll work."

I bite back my protest, squashing the urge to convince him that Henrietta would be a worthy friend, and nod.

"Maybe Malik and I can find some pretty canisters and pick up some tea for you. It could look really good, if we stage it right."

His nod is curt, and he leaves the room abruptly, without another word.

Malik smiles. "We'll wear him down eventually."

"You think?"

"Yeah. That's the most he's talked to anyone outside the family in weeks. And it was his idea, to ask you what you thought. He likes you."

I snort. "That's what it looks like when he likes someone?"

He chuckles. "Yeah. Sometimes he straight up ignores people. Acts like they're not in the room."

I walk to the window, letting my fingers trail along the fabric of the two chairs sitting in the sunlight. "Has he always been this way?"

"No. I guess when people betray you, it changes you, you know? He's not the same as he used to be."

"Oh," I say, my mouth going dry.

Add yet another reason Malik can never find out who I really am.

Three hours later, I'm glancing nervously at my phone, checking the time. It's past six. Malik and I spent the time arranging some of the smaller stuff that arrived under the silent watch of Charles, whose only acknowledgment of our actions came from the occasional approving nod when he liked how I put things.

Charles. I think of him as Charles now. That's sort of weird. But I can't think of him as some fancy-shmancy CEO anymore. He's just Malik's grandpa.

And now I'm screwed. Alex's mom is going to be home by the time we get there. What if Malik tries to walk me to the door? And Alex's mom is there and calls me Holiday . . . or asks what I'm doing at their house? Or says, *Oh, hey, nice to see you, Alex isn't home yet*?

And why is Malik driving so freaking slowly? What happened to race-car driver Malik? There's a chance we could still beat her, if she made any stops on her way home from work.

"Um, take a right up here," I say, pointing to Garfield Street.

He turns, and the car is bathed in the shadows of the oak trees lining the sides of the road.

Alex lives in an older part of town. The homes are spaced out, all beautiful turn-of-the-century houses with big wraparound porches and sparkling white shutters. The landscaping is lush and mature, and most houses—including Alex's—have a view of the lake. These might not hold a candle to Malik's mansion, but again, they're well into the seven figures, so that's good enough for my cover story.

"It's the blue one on the right up here."

He pulls up to the curb, and I bite back a sigh of relief as I realize Alex's mom's car is not in the driveway. I don't know if it's the traffic gods or something else, but this could still work.

"Thanks for the ride home. I really appreciate it," I say, unbuckling and pushing the door open. "See you later!" I bound out of the car, fingering the key in my pocket. *Home free.*

"Wait up," he calls out. "I can at least walk you to your door."

Ugh. *Not* home free. I stop on the front lawn, holding in a breath. "You don't have to do that."

"Don't be silly," he says, stepping out of the car and up onto the sidewalk.

"Um, thanks." Of course he's chivalrous. Of course.

We walk toward the porch and I position the key in my hand so that I can slide it right in and get inside and he can just *go away*. But as we step up onto the enormous wooden porch, a car engine hums behind us, growing louder.

Oh, man.

Alex's mom is home.

"Okay, got home safe, thanks!" I say, rushing to the front door.

"Is that your mom?"

I purse my lips, closing my eyes as I count to three before turning around to face him. "Um, yep! She's kinda in a rush today, though, as she had some big projects at work and everything. Besides, I'm not really supposed to have boys over, so—"

But she's already getting out of the car, taking in me and Malik just hanging out on her front porch and glancing over to his sparking silver car. She presses a button on her keys, and the trunk of her car pops and rises to show a bunch of white plastic grocery-store bags. She hardly takes her eyes off us as she pulls a few of the bags and a gallon of milk out of the car.

If I don't think fast, she's going to step up on this porch and ask what I'm doing here.

"Groceries?" I practically shout. "I can help you bring in groceries!" I rush across the lawn, scrambling to come up with some way this can be turned around.

She can't call me by my real name.

She can't reference Alex in a way that makes Malik realize this is *Alex's house*.

She can't treat me like I'm *not* her daughter.

I almost groan aloud when I see how many bags are in the trunk, definitely more than Alex's mom and I can carry in one trip. This is why she was late. She went full-blown grocery shopping. And knowing Malik . . .

"Let me give you a hand with this," he says, right on time, reaching in and scooping up a few bags.

No, no, no. He has to leave.

Alex's mom is just standing there, one eyebrow raised, glancing between me, Malik, and his car at the curb. She's never met any boy I've been interested in, and surely she must wonder how it is that I've snared the attention of a boy with a car quite that shiny.

And what the heck we're both doing hanging out in front of the house.

"This is Malik," I say brightly. "He was just dropping me off."

"Oh, is Alex—"

"She's not here yet," I say. *Here. Here* is safe. *Home* is not. "She's on her way, though."

"Okay."

And that's how the three of us end up walking inside together, grocery bags in hand, Malik clearly taking in the space.

He pauses as he passes the mantel, as if to study the frames perched on top.

The frames holding family photos!

"Can't let that ice cream melt!" I practically shout, bumping into his back and shoving him past the fireplace. He stumbles forward and glances back at me, surprise playing across his features, but doesn't ask what the heck my problem is.

The kitchen is light and bright, with antique-white cabinets, black marble countertops, and industrial-grade stainless appliances. Once we deposit the bags on the kitchen table, and Alex's mom has gone outside to grab another load, I twist around and hook my arm into Malik's like I'm escorting him down the aisle.

"I'd give you the grand tour, but I'm sure you're busy."

"Actually, I'd love one," he says. "Old places like this are pretty cool. No wonder you're into history, if you grew up in a place like this."

Curses. I can't give him a freaking tour of Alex's house!

"Um, okay," I say. This is about to be the world's worst home tour. "So you already saw the kitchen and the living room," I say, tugging him through it without giving him a moment to stop and admire the crown moldings, the hand-scraped hardwood, or the antique brocade couch. Alex's mom cannot see me giving him this tour. She'll be like, *What the heck are you doing? You can't just bring a random boy in here and start showing him my house.*

"The bedrooms are upstairs. I, um, can't show you my mom's room or anything—she's private—but you can see mine."

As the words leave my mouth and I begin to lead him up the stairs, I think of all the things in Alex's room that are nothing like me. Stuff that could tip him off.

Soccer trophies. I can pretend I'm into soccer.

And then there's the plain white furniture and a blue comforter.

Plus all those ribbons from sixth grade when she decided to do 4-H with her dog.

As I shove open the door, I remember the most obvious thing of all: The big block letters we painted a couple of years back and mounted on a big board still hanging on the wall over the doorway. Letters spelling out: ALEXANDRIA.

My mouth goes dry as he steps into the room, the name emblazoned right over his head. As long as he doesn't turn around . . .

"Look at that!" I shout, pushing him toward the window. "It's such a beautiful day! Just take in that view!"

Malik starts to glance back as if to ask why I'm essentially hollering at him, but I give him a little shove, and he obeys, walking toward the window.

We're okay as long as he doesn't turn back toward me.

Except . . . it's not like I can expect him to walk backward when we leave the room.

I rush forward, flinging open the window. "My mom has the best view, but if you lean out the window and look far to your right, you can see the lake. You really gotta lean out though."

He obeys, putting his hands on the windowsill and leaning forward.

I backpedal as quickly as I can, like a crab on speed, and leap at the sign over Alex's door.

It doesn't come down easy. There's a single screw at the top, in the middle, holding it up. I glance over my shoulder, and Malik is still hanging out the window, so I yank harder.

And it gives, raining drywall dust down on me as the screw yanks out of the wall. The board is in my hand as I sputter, spitting out the white, chalky dust I've inhaled.

Malik is sliding back, out of the window.

"Look at that bird!" I practically scream. "It's like a pterodactyl!"

He jumps, knocking his head on the top of the window frame, just as I fling the board into the closet. As I slide the door shut, he turns around, wincing as he rubs the back of his head.

"Oh gosh, I'm sorry, I didn't mean to make you hit your head. It was just . . . a really big bird. Like Big Bird!" Geez, I sound like an idiot. "Except, you know, not yellow."

"It's okay," he says, finally dropping his hand from his head. "I think I'll survive."

"Great," I say brightly. "So anyway, this is my room, and I probably shouldn't keep you much—"

The door behind me swings open, and my stomach sinks as Alex bursts into the room. "So my mom texted me, and she said—"

Alex's voice cuts off when she sees Malik standing beside me.

"Uh, hey," she says. How did she not see his car out on the curb?

I give her a crazy smile, like I'm excited to see her. "So, I was just showing Malik *my room*," I say.

Alex's eyes immediately dart to the spot above the door, pausing when she comes across the big hole in her wall, her lips parting.

"That's great," she says, recovering, glancing down at spot of white drywall dust on her carpet. "But did you forget we had plans? You know, to go to . . . that thing we were invited to?"

"Oh," I say, wringing my hands. "I guess I did! We should really get going. To, the, uh, thing, since we RSVP'd and all." I walk toward Alex, hoping Malik follows. "Sorry, I mean, I really just forgot about our big plans."

But for a long moment, he doesn't move. Just stares at me, his eyebrows knitted as he chews on the edge of his lip. His perfect, glorious lip that I am never going to kiss again if he figures me out.

Wow, am I bad at this. Improv looks so much easier on TV.

"Uh, okay. I need to head out anyway," he says.

"Mm-hmm," I say. "Let me walk you out."

The three of us descend the stairs, my hand gliding down the oak bannister, relief slowly setting in. I've done it!

Halfway across the living room, Alex's mom steps into the doorway to the kitchen. "Did you want to stay for dinner, Holi—"

"Orange juice!" Alexandria shouts over the top of *day*.

Malik stops and raises a brow, glancing over at me with a total WTF look.

"I am dying for orange juice!" she shouts again, rushing across the living room. She disappears into the kitchen, pulling her mother along with her, presumably to engage her in a scintillating conversation about orange juice.

"Um, yeah. Alex has a thing about vitamin C," I say feebly as I usher Malik out of the house.

We walk over to his car, and I stop at the curb. "Um, so I guess we should go tea shopping sometime?"

He laughs, pulling me close for a hug. When we pull apart, he pauses, with scarcely an inch to separate us. "I think that can be arranged."

"Great. Text me later?"

He turns me so I'm leaning back against his car and he has one hand propped up beside my shoulder. Then he leans in slowly, agonizingly so, until my eyes slip shut and he kisses me.

He pulls away just enough for our eyelashes to practically brush each other and meets my gaze.

"Until next time?"

"Mm-hmm," is all I can muster, hypnotized by his eyes.

He finally steps away, leaving me almost gasping for breath. I move away from his car and step onto Alex's front lawn, waving good-bye as he climbs into his car and pulls away.

That boy kisses like a god.

CHAPTER FIFTEEN

Malik and I are at the mall, of all places. I guess I thought people as obscenely wealthy as his family only shopped on, like, Rodeo Drive or something. But here we are at Nordstrom, surveying the racks.

"She likes purple," he says, tipping his head to the side and staring at a scarf.

"Do you really think she wants a scarf?" I ask, looking at the item in his hands.

"No, but what else am I supposed to get her?" He scrubs at his hair with his hands.

"I don't know," I say, kind of loving how stressed out he is about getting his mom a birthday present. He's so rarely this . . . ruffled. "I've never met your mom."

"I know."

"Do you have any pictures of you guys together over the years? Like on a computer or something?"

He looks up. "Uh, yeah."

"You could order something personalized. Parents totally dig that stuff. Make her a scrapbook or framed photos or something. So she can hang it in her office and brag about you."

He looks up at me, surprised. "She'd love that."

"Awesome. You can do that from your computer at home and have it shipped to her. And we can pick out a card or something, for a more personalized touch."

"Perfect."

"Good. Now let's go hit up the food court. I'm dying for a Slurpee."

We leave the store behind, stepping back into the bright, tall corridors of the mall. Overhead, big skylights show it's still raining outside, drops pounding against the glass and the clouds a dark and menacing gray.

We're just passing a staircase, Malik walking beside me and kind of swinging my hand back and forth.

"Mathews!"

I freeze at the familiar voice and the nickname, dread making my limbs feel heavy.

Hunter always did call everyone by their last name. He claims it's from years of playing soccer and basketball with two coaches who referred to every player that way. It drove me crazy because it always made me feel like he thought of me as one of the guys.

Today is the first time I've ever been grateful for that quirk of his.

I turn around to see him jogging down the steps, taking them two by two. He's going so fast, I half expect him to trip on his own feet and tumble down the stairs.

Malik leans in. "Who's that?"

"Uh, an old boyfriend," I say, the words floating out on a whisper. I give him a feeble smile as Hunter approaches.

As he rushes over to us, I realize he's staring at Malik and not me, his eyes raking over him from head to toe as if sizing up his replacement. Only when he's a foot away does he suddenly switch his focus, throwing his arms around me in an abrupt, unwelcome hug. I reluctantly let go of Malik's hand to halfheartedly hug him back, awkwardly tapping on his back a few times as if to cry uncle.

"Um. Hi, Hunter," I say, trying to untangle myself from his way-too-strong hug. "This is Malik. Malik, this is Hunter."

Malik starts to extend his hand, and then Hunter's jutting out his fist, and Malik is forced to turn what should've been a handshake into a very bro-ish fist bump.

Malik looks ridiculous when he fist-bumps. Like he's painfully unaccustomed to it.

"You guys serious?" Hunter says, glancing back at me again, his eyes sparkling with intrigue.

It's not like Hunter broke up with me yesterday. It's been months. "That stopped being your business last April. How's Finley, by the way?"

Hunter shrugs but doesn't meet my gaze. "Eh, I don't know. Fine, I guess," he says, dismissing my question. "So how'd you two meet?"

Ugh. Where's one of those toy helicopters people are always playing with at mall kiosks? If only one could crash straight into Hunter's face.

"Oh, you know . . . ," I say, waving away the question. I turn to Malik, trying to send him my best let's-get-out-of-this-now look.

"No, actually, I don't know. What kind of places do you guys hang out at?" he asks, his gaze sliding over Malik. Slowly, like he's assessing a rival in a boxing ring.

Something about the question hits me the wrong way. Suddenly, I'm deeply uncomfortable, eager to get away from the weird, digging questions. Why is he so worried about me being with Malik? I haven't talked to Hunter in months. He shouldn't care. Not like this.

"Again, none of your business, actually. And anyway, I think we need to get going," I say, glancing at Malik for help. "We have plans today, so . . ."

"Yeah, we're about to be late. Was nice to meet you, um—" Malik pauses and shrugs as if he can't remember Hunter's name. It's clear he's also taken stock of Hunter and doesn't particularly like what he sees.

"Hunter," he supplies. "You sure you have to go? Maybe we could—"

"Yep, we're in a real rush, sorry," I say. "We'll just have to catch up some other time, okay?" I take Malik's hand again, and we rush off, leaving Hunter to stand in the middle of the corridor, watching us longingly.

"Ugh, so that was . . . ," I say, my voice trailing off. "Uh, really, really weird. I don't know why he was so enthralled by you."

"It's not that weird," Malik says, glancing at me from the corner of his eye. He doesn't seem surprised. More . . . resigned.

"Huh? I mean, he's into girls," I say, offering a nervous laugh. "Let me just clear that up for you."

"He recognized me," Malik says simply, his lips turned down a little as he shrugs.

"I'm not sure why he had to stare at your watch and—"

I go silent when his statement sinks in.

"Oh." I swallow. *"Oh."*

That's when I finally understand.

He knows who Malik is. Not *Malik*, but *Malik Buchannan*, billionaire. The guy from *Time*, TMZ, *Forbes* . . .

The *pre*-Nepal Malik.

Hunter barely looked at me, instead stealing looks at Malik, as if he needed to memorize each detail—not just his silver Rolex, but his perfectly polished black leather shoes . . . his scarf . . .

It was like he was cataloging it for later to check just how expensive everything Malik was wearing might be.

"Oh," I say again. "Is this what it's like?" I ask, glancing around the mall, wondering who else recognizes him, and seeing the other shoppers in a whole new light.

"More or less, yeah."

"I thought he was jealous of you. You know, checking you out since you're the first guy he's seen me with since we broke up. But it's the opposite. He's jealous of *me* for being around you, isn't he?"

Malik shrugs, stuffing his hands into his pockets.

"He pretty much wanted to glom onto you."

"Yeah. I don't know where people think that will get them, but it happens."

"A lot?"

"More often than not. It used to amuse me, but that was before."

I don't have to ask what *before* he means.

"Well, if it makes you feel better, Hunter's got the IQ of a block of wood, so you wouldn't want him in your life anyway."

Malik cracks a smile then, hooking his arm around my shoulder and pulling me up against the length of his body. "Thanks."

"Hey, anytime you need someone to insult Hunter, I'm your girl."

Malik slings his arms around my shoulders, squeezing me closer. "No, I mean thanks for not being like him. And like a thousand others."

"Anytime," I say.

And, as I let myself enjoy the weight of his arm around me, I try not to notice the lady on the second-floor balcony, recording us on her cell phone.

CHAPTER SIXTEEN

On days like today, I kind of wish I had a window seat in my bedroom. It's pouring, and water streams down the window so thickly, I can barely see the blurry outlines of trees.

The apartment is silent. My mom's down the hall in her office, meeting with an advertising agency to create a new brochure she thinks will bring in more new residents.

I never noticed how softly I can hear the rain in here. It's so well insulated, compared to every other place we've lived, that it's almost like watching and listening to rain on TV. Like I'm separated from it.

I step back, trying not to cringe at the print my forehead has left behind on the glass, and head out of the door of our apartment. It's way too yucky to go outside and actually *do* anything, so I may as well make myself useful and earn a few more extra bucks for my college fund. I head back to the front desk, hoping the receptionist has had some calls requesting my help. I'm down to barely a month before I leave, and every dollar will help.

Julia's not at her desk, though. I glance up and down the hall, waiting for her to appear, but she's nowhere to be seen.

I flip her book open, skimming down a page of scribbles to see if my name pops out on any pages.

Room 405. Says the shades on her window are stuck.

405. Henrietta. The time is two hours ago, but it's worth double-checking that someone helped her. She doesn't tip me, since she thinks I'm family, but it doesn't mean I don't want to help her.

I'm inside the elevator, and just as the doors start to ease shut, a hand juts into the crack, and they slide open again.

Malik grins. "You," he says.

"Me," I reply, grinning.

"Our superb grandchildren skills are really in sync," he jokes.

Like it's such a crazy coincidence that he runs into me almost every time he's here.

"Yep," I say.

The door slips shut, and he moves over, his hand dangling down beside mine, and interlaces our fingers, giving mine a squeeze. "Let's go to dinner or something tonight."

Warmth spirals through me at the casual way he's saying it. It's amazing how fast things evolved between us and became comfortable.

The doors click open, and we walk into the hall, our fingers slipping apart as we arrive at the spot where we must go in different directions. He pauses. "So, text me when you're done visiting and we'll figure something out?"

"Sure," I say. I head to Henrietta's door, knocking twice as Malik heads down the hall to his grandpa's place.

Silence.

Behind me, the sound of the fancy family-crest brass knocker echoes down the hall. I glance back, to see if he's noticed I'm still here, and his eyes are trained on me.

"Not home?" he asks.

"Nah, she's usually just a little slow to get to the door," I say, waving away his look. "Don't wait on me."

But now he's walking away from his grandpa's place and striding toward me. He's halfway there when Charles opens the door, and Malik hesitates.

"Seriously, go on," I say, making a ridiculous shooing motion. Ugh, I am being way too obvious. "I'll catch up with you later."

I turn away from the door because there's no denying nobody is going to answer it and head back in the direction of the elevator.

"Hey, why don't you come on in? He had some of Cartwell's art put up. Pollack, I think?"

I hesitate. He's said the magic words.

"You know you want to," he fairly singsongs.

I spin back around and stride down the hall, hoping my mom doesn't suddenly get the urge to check on the fourth-floor residents, and slip into Charles's apartment.

"Wow," I say breathlessly, stepping closer.

"She's beautiful," Charles replies from somewhere behind me, the pride positively dripping from his words. "Isn't she?"

His voice is nearly as breathless as my own, and I know without a doubt he appreciates the beauty of it with the same passion I do.

Who would have thought I'd have anything in common with Charles Buchannan?

"But it's so close to the windows. The sunlight—"

"I've already arranged for UV-blocking blinds," he says.

I turn and grin at him. "Smart."

"So are you," he says simply, walking away and leaving me gaping.

After all his aloofness, after all his gruffness, he tells me I'm *smart*.

It's only when I follow his trek across the room that I take in the rest of the items he's so carefully arranged. The sideboards, the Fabergé, the vase. Everything Malik and I chose has arrived.

"So, Grandpa, I thought we could finally go down to one of the restaurants for lunch," Malik says, turning to his grandfather.

"No," he says, the word flat and insistent.

"Come on, you can't stay up here forever. There's a whole world out there."

"Who cares?"

"Look, if you don't want to do it for you, do it for me. Mom's been on my case to get you out of here. She's driving me crazy."

"My eating down there won't stop her from her ridiculous worries. She should be focusing on the business instead of my social calendar."

"Oh, come on, it's just one lunch," I say. "And maybe that'll get her off his back for a week or two. That's worth it, right?"

He groans, rolling his eyes. But I can see it. We've worn him down.

"Fine, then. But only if you come too," Charles says, waving his hand in my direction. "You're the only one who talks about anything interesting."

"Oh, I wouldn't want to intrude," I say, backing up as if a few feet of extra space will extrapolate me from the quicksand I've landed in. I can't sit in the dining hall with them, surrounded by all the residents. "And, um, I've got things to—"

"Oh, come on," Malik says, turning to me. His eyes are pleading. And I know it's for his grandfather's sake, not his own. He needs me to do this. "Henrietta's not even home, so you've got some free time. Come with us."

And that's how I find myself holding the elbow of Charles Buchannan, hoping an earthquake happens before we get to the dining room, or that all the people inside forget what my name is.

Simultaneously.

We have to pass my mom's office as we head to the dining hall, and she catches a glimpse of us as I step by her windows.

She opens her mouth, as if to call out to me, but then it just kind of hangs there as she takes in whose arm I'm holding.

She should be mad, since we kind of agreed I'd stay away from Charles, but judging by her expression, she's too excited to see him down here to care.

I give her a I-have-no-idea-what-I'm-doing-and-heeeeeelllllp look, but she doesn't seem to notice. Probably because she's beaming as we turn toward the dining room. I bet in two-point-five seconds, she picks up the phone to call Malik's mom and tell her about how Charles has come out of his shell and is dining with his neighbors.

If she knew my identity—and thus, her job—hung by such a precarious thread, she wouldn't be so excited.

"Holiday," Mrs. Hannigan, the lady who gave me all her old doilies, calls out and my stomach drops into my knees. *No, no, no, no, no.* Five seconds into the dining hall and I'm going to have to drag out my ridiculous story again.

Malik is going to think I'm insane when he sees just how big my supposed holiday-loving reputation is.

"Where ya been hiding lately?"

Malik raises a brow at me, and my heart revolts, feeling like it's trying to climb up my throat.

"Um, you know, just busy!" I say to her, steering Mr. Buchannan in the opposite direction. I can't miss the way Malik stares, and I know he's wondering if my "holiday obsession" is a little out of hand.

"I'll catch up with you later, okay?" I call over my shoulder. I meet Malik's gaze, shrugging. "My, um, grandma has lived here a long time, so I know a lot of the residents super well. Sometimes I help other people decorate for holidays, too. It's one of those my-reputation-precedes-me sort of things, if you know what I mean."

I bring Charles and Malik toward one of the smaller tables, near a window, just far enough removed from the rest of the diners that it'll put off anyone else in the room trying to talk to us.

I pull out a chair for Charles, one that will give him a nice view of the lake but puts his back to the crowds, so he doesn't get overwhelmed. He hangs his cane on the edge of the table and sits down, studying the place settings.

I hope he knows how to use them, because I sure don't.

"This silver is rather shoddy," Charles says, holding up a fork. "Does no one polish it?"

I swallow. "Um, mine looks pretty sparkly," I say. "I'm sure someone polishes it."

A waitress swoops in then, filling our water glasses and saving me from more talk of silverware.

Charles doesn't speak until the waitress leaves, and then he peers down his nose at the menu. "Have you eaten here before?"

"Yes, a few times," I lie. I don't know what most of the words on the menu even mean, so I've always picked one of the other two on-site restaurant options to eat at. But I know enough about the restaurant to fake it. "Um, they've received two Michelin stars. The food is very good."

"Hmph," he says, flipping the page of the menu.

I don't know what else to say, so I open up my own leather-bound menu and study it. As I pretend to read, the table falls awkwardly silent. I'll just let them order first and say, "Me too," and then hope I don't hate it.

"I was thinking we could go to an art auction," Charles says abruptly.

"Really?" Malik says, his shock evident. "That would be amazing."

Has Charles really not left his place at all? It's been weeks since we went and bought the Goya. How could he just . . . stay inside his apartment? I mean, sure, his place is big, but if he doesn't even come downstairs for the recreational stuff, doesn't he get stir crazy?

"You too," Charles says, nodding in my direction. "You can choose which one."

My jaw drops. "You want me to pick an auction for you?"

"You were right about *The Nude Maja*, weren't you? I've been out of the art world too long. Find me something exciting, and maybe I'll go."

I can tell by Malik's stunned reaction that this is the most outgoing he's been in months . . . maybe longer. When I don't reply, Malik nudges my ankle with the toe of his shoe.

"Oh, um, yes!" I say, realizing I'm just sitting here, gaping. "That would be great. I would be happy to find you something. What are you looking for?"

He shrugs. "Something grand to hang over the fireplace."

"Sure. Yes. Definitely. I can find something with paintings." I don't even know if that's true—I don't know how to find something *worthy* of Charles Buchannan.

"Hello!" comes a voice, and the screeching of a chair.

I look up to find Henrietta taking the fourth, empty seat, beaming from ear to ear.

"Heyyyy," I say, dragging out the word as I churn through all the ways the next few moments could go. I smile as wide as I can, glancing over at Charles. I don't know if the extra company will set him off.

He is sitting perfectly still, staring at Henrietta as she carefully slides into the chair.

"Uh, may I introduce you to Mr. Charles Buchannan?" I ask, nodding in his direction. "He's the new resident on your floor. And this is his grandson, Malik."

She smiles, wide and warm, in that way only Henrietta can. I hope I'm half as chipper and outgoing as she is when I get to be her age.

Charles nods curtly in her direction.

But Henrietta is, as ever, oblivious to any verbal coldness. She grabs the linen napkin, smoothing it across her lap. "What is your favorite place in the world, Charles?"

"What?" he snaps, suspicion flaring in his eyes. "What kind of question is that?"

"She asks everyone that," I explain, glancing over at Malik to find him pursing his lips in amusement. Now he knows I wasn't kidding when I said I got my little question from Henrietta.

"It's more interesting than asking what you do for a living," Henrietta adds. "Especially at our age. Don't you think?"

Charles sort of leans back in his chair, as if caught off guard by Henrietta's forwardness. Or maybe it's because he's spent his life being defined by his company, and Henrietta has clearly expressed that she finds being defined by your career uninteresting.

Henrietta beams. "Mine is Venice," she explains.

Surprise blooms across Charles's face. "I love Venice. I have a vacation home there, on Calle Del Scaleter."

Henrietta grins. "There's a great restaurant on that street. They serve the best gnocchi I've ever had. It's called—"

"Da Fiore," they say simultaneously.

When Charles smiles, wide and bright, it's all I can do to keep my jaw from dropping.

"You've been there," Henrietta says.

"Every time I visit," he says.

"It's worth the long wait for a table," Henrietta replies.

"The best things in life are worth the wait," he says.

There's a spark of interest in his eyes, and for the first time, I realize that maybe my mom was right about him needing this place.

Maybe if he realizes the residents aren't just put out to pasture—they're interesting people with full lives—he'll come out of his shell. Maybe this is just one lunch, but it's a step in the right direction.

If I can keep dragging him out of his apartment, he'll realize Sunrise House is pretty awesome, and he'll stay. . . .

And my mom's job will be secure.

CHAPTER SEVENTEEN

A week later, I follow Malik down a long corridor, my low heels clicking on the glossy hardwood, my fingers wrapped around a thin paper booklet. I *really* hope this auction doesn't suck. It was the only thing on the Mozak and Klein schedule. I figured if they had the pull to put together an auction for Roger Cartwell, they probably sold other awesome stuff.

"Slow down," Charles grumbles behind me. My step falters as a blush blooms across my cheeks. How could I forget he has a freaking *cane*?

Malik just flashes him a grin. "I thought you wanted time to read the catalog before they started."

Charles harrumphs, as if to admit that Malik is right but he doesn't like it.

"Dad," a voice calls out, and I glance over Malik's shoulder to see a stunning woman with wavy black hair stepping out of the room we were heading to. Her long, slim legs and stiletto heels gobble up the distance between us, and I'm so awestruck by her wide-eyed, model-good-looks that it takes a moment for the truth to hit me.

If she called Charles *Dad*, that mean's she's . . .

"Mom," Malik says, "I thought you couldn't make it."

As she steps up closer to us, she starts to speak, but then her eyes land on me and she turns away from her son.

"Lucy, I presume?" She flashes me a dazzling smile that clearly conveys she's excited to meet me, and extends her hand.

She knows my name.

No, wait, that's not my name.

"Yep, that's me," I say brightly, extending my hand. "Nice to meet you . . ."

"Patricia," she offers. "Patricia Buchannan. It's so nice to finally meet the girl who has inspired my father."

Charles huffs beside us but says nothing.

"Oh, I mean, I don't know about that," I say, shyness suddenly overwhelming me. "I really didn't *do* anything."

"Well," she says brightly, the smile never leaving her face, "that painting you found certainly woke him up. So I owe you a big thank-you."

"Um, okay," I say meekly, fighting the urge to look over at Charles. He must be embarrassed by this, right? He doesn't seem to like people judging him, picking him apart. Even I know that. "Uh, you're welcome."

"I saved us some seats," she says, turning back to her father. "Middle of the room, just like you like."

Malik and I swap a glance, and I know he's remembering my insistence on our date to sit in the middle of the room. So maybe Charles and I have art *and* seating preferences in common.

"Let's get on with it, then," Charles says, waving his hand at her like a pesky fly. In that instant, I know I was right and his daughter's words have embarrassed him.

Patricia takes Charles's elbow, and they walk into the room ahead of us, making their way toward a row of seats in the middle. Malik and I trail after, our hands clasped.

"Malik!" someone calls out, the voice soft, feminine, and a little too high-pitched.

His fingers slip from mine as we both turn toward the voice.

A petite redhead with vibrant green eyes grins, flinging her arms around him and forcing me to step back or get smacked in the face. "It's so great to see you!"

She does the whole air-kisses-on-his-cheek thing that I've only ever seen on TV, then steps back to smile at him.

She studies him, blinking demurely as she fingers an enormous diamond pendant. The kind of diamond that people look for in wrecked ships or something. The kind of thing that could pay for four years of college with money left over.

Whoever this girl is, she's not removed from Malik's world.

"You've been hiding from me, haven't you?"

He laughs uncomfortably. "Of course not."

She pouts, reaching out to run her finger down his arm. "You didn't return my last call."

I take a tiny, involuntary step back, immediately wondering if he ever reserved whole movie theaters for *her*.

Her eyes flit to me, as if she hadn't seen me standing beside him until now, and her hand goes back to the diamond pendant. Her eyes narrow, until I can barely see them between her thick, curly lashes. "I'm sorry, have we met?"

"I don't believe we have," I say, trying to keep my voice level to pretend this girl doesn't intimidate me.

"Oh, I'm sorry," Malik says. "Lucy, this is my friend Emma. Emma, this is my girlfriend, Lucy."

I nearly gasp out loud.

My girlfriend. Oh my god, he just introduced me as his girl-friend! I'm about to start spinning in circles and singing, *"The hills are aliiiive,"* when reality hits.

Hard.

I'm not supposed to be his girlfriend. I'm his *fling.* This is casual. Completely, totally casual.

I reach a hand out, pretending not to notice that her freckled face seems to have paled. "Nice to meet you."

She makes no move to accept my outstretched hand. Instead, her eyes sweep over me, and I'm suddenly, entirely grateful for Alex's clothes. They might not be Armani or Gucci or whatever this girl is probably wearing, but they'll do.

"Likewise," she says, but there's no truth behind the words.

I drop my hand, realizing I've left it sticking out about three heartbeats too long. I don't know what to do with it since I have no pockets and no fancy diamond necklace to play with.

Malik saves me, his fingers finding mine and giving them a squeeze.

The shift in her is almost imperceptible, but it's there: the flash of self-doubt, the slightest pink tinge to her cheeks.

Behind us—at the front of the big ballroom, someone speaks. "If you could please find your seats," the man says, "we'll get things started."

"Well, it was nice to see you again," Malik says, pulling me away without bothering to glance back at her.

"It was *so* lovely to meet you," I add, almost feeling sorry for her.

Almost.

"Thank you," Malik whispers, his words hot on my ear.

"Anytime," I respond, trying not to analyze his gratitude and failing.

What's he thanking me for? Not overreacting to meeting his Barbie-perfect ex? Pretending to be his girlfriend? Is that what happened back there? Did he actually mean it when he called me his girlfriend?

"I need to talk to you for a minute," he says, pulling me in the opposite direction of our seats, back toward the door we originally came through.

We navigate upstream through the crush of people decked out in fancy suits and gold watches and tailored skirts moving to find their seats. I don't miss the curious glances, the ladies whose eyes rake over Malik and then me in turn. I get the overwhelming sense that they all know him and he's their golden boy.

The hallway is empty and unusually quiet. My heels echo down the hall.

Malik faces me, his lips curling into an adorably boyish smile. "Sorry you had to meet her."

"She seemed *delightful*," I joke.

He chuckles, reaching out to tuck a strand of hair behind my ear. I have an overwhelming urge to close my eyes and lean into his touch.

"At the urging of my mother, I went on one date with her six months ago. I haven't been able to get rid of her since."

"Why? Does your mom like her?"

He shrugs. "Emma's father is a senator, and she's going to go to med school. It made sense, at first. I thought she'd get what I wanted to do. Why else would she want to become a doctor, if not to help people? But it wasn't about that. It was about the prestige and the title. I don't even know if she's going to practice medicine after graduation, or if she just wants to put a few letters behind her name."

"Oh."

"But that wasn't why I needed to talk to you."

"Okay . . . ," I say.

He glances back at the room we just left, as if he doesn't want to be overheard. But when he turns back to face me, I realize it's not about that at all.

He's nervous.

"It's just . . . when I introduced you to her, I didn't mean to call you my girlfriend. It slipped out."

Oh my god. That's why he's nervous. He's backpedaling, trying to retract the label. The label I'm not supposed to want. I look down at the floor, feeling like I just went from zero to sixty and back again. I don't want to acknowledge my disappointment. This is good, that he doesn't want to be boyfriend and girlfriend.

We're never supposed to label it. *Flings* don't have labels.

"Hey. Look at me."

I glance up at him, trying not to betray my thoughts. I force the best smile I can muster.

"The thing is, as soon as I said the words . . ." He steps closer, so that there's scarcely an inch between us, and I have to tip my head back to look up into his eyes. "I realized I wanted it to be true. I want you to be my girlfriend."

Emotions wage war in my chest. I'm thrilled and scared, flattered and worried. But when I look at the sincerity and the hopefulness splayed across his face, there's no way I can reject him.

"Okay," I say. As the word slips out, I feel both relieved and guilty.

This can still be a fling. Being his girlfriend isn't that big of a deal, right? There's less than a month until I leave. It's not like this little label will mean that much in the grand scheme of things.

He grins so widely, his pearly white teeth flash. "Yes, you'll be with me? Exclusively?"

"Yes," I say, unable wipe the smile from my face. "Yes, I'll be your girlfriend."

"Great. Now let's go watch my grandfather buy an obscene amount of art."

Two hours later, I'm standing on an observation deck outside the auction house, staring out across the water. Beside me, Charles leans on his cane.

Malik went to grab some coffee while his mother went to pay for the painting Charles purchased, leaving me alone with Charles and trying to feel out whether he's enjoyed his day. He's . . . oddly silent.

Until he's not.

"That's our building, you know," he says, motioning to a tower in the distance.

"The tall one, right?"

"Yes. Tallest building in Bellevue." Pride drips from his voice. "Even the materials used in the facility are American made. The steel, the flooring, the fixtures . . . everything."

"Is that how your daughter's real estate projects are done?"

"Of course. I wouldn't allow her to be part of the company if she would do it any other way."

"You must be very proud of all you've accomplished," I say.

"I am," he replies simply.

I glance over at him from the corner of my eye, trying to discern his mood. He's chattier than normal, not quite as guarded. It's almost like the art auction was what he needed to draw him out of his curmudgeon shell.

"Does it bother you, not going there every day?"

His lips thin, and he doesn't speak, just gives me a curt nod.

"If your daughter aligns so well with the vision of the company . . . why isn't she the one sitting in your office? Why isn't she your voice in the boardroom?"

His eyes narrow, and his gaze drifts over me. And I feel like *we* are the ones in the board room, and he's appraising his opponent. "She may do that. The real estate branch has grown to the point that it warrants a position on the board. I'm proud of what she's done."

"Malik wants you to be proud of him, too, you know," I say. "But he also needs space to figure out what he wants to do."

"There's nothing to figure out. He'll make an excellent CEO."

"Did you enjoy it?" I ask. "Sitting at that desk?"

"Of course I did," he says, scoffing like it's a stupid question.

"What did you love about it?"

"A thousand things. I was good at it. What I did mattered. I watched it come together, brick by brick, year by year."

I turn away from the railing and lean my hip against the steel and glass. "But all those things . . . they're *your* reasons. What reason does Malik have to want to become you?"

"He doesn't need to *become* me," Charles says. But there's no bite to his tone. He's actually open to having this conversation, with is enough to throw me off. Somehow I've won him over, been accepted into his small circle of trusted people. He's talking to me like this conversation matters . . . like maybe my opinion matters.

"But that's what you want from him."

"No, what I mean is . . . he doesn't *need* to become me, because we're already the same."

I narrow my eyes. "What do you mean?"

"I mean . . ." The edge of his lip curls up. "He's exactly like me. Exactly like his mom. He wants to create something himself. He wants to build it from scratch and watch it grow. And that's something I understand."

"So why is it not okay with you?" Malik's voice comes from behind me. I startle and blush. I don't know how much he heard, but it feels like I've overstepped my bounds, talking to his grandfather like this.

Malik stops a few feet shy of his grandfather, and studies him, staring into his eyes. "Why can't I start something myself? Watch it grow, *brick by brick*?"

Okay, then. He definitely overheard more than the last few words of my conversation with Charles.

Charles stares at Malik for a long moment, one that stretches on and on. And then, finally, he says, "Just tell me what you want to build. And I'll give you the bricks."

A lump grows in my throat, caused by the mixture of joy and shock and . . . a little bit of worry, because even with his grandfather's blessing, Malik doesn't know what it is he wants to build.

But then I see Malik's megawatt smile.

And the first hug I've ever witnessed between the Buchannan boys, the most beautiful thing in the world.

And all I can do is hope that he figures it out.

Because Charles isn't the roadblock we thought he was.

CHAPTER EIGHTEEN

The next day, my phone chirps.

We have a problem.

That's all that's in the text Alex sends me. I sit down at my desk, my stomach twisting as I grip my phone tightly in my hand.

What? Call me.

Can't. In the car with my mom. She's talking on Bluetooth to a client and it's going on forever.

Okay . . . elaborate on the problem, I say, my fingers flying across the keyboard. Oh god, what if they, like, just left the grocery store after running into Malik and now he's wondering why my BFF hangs out with my "mom" when I'm not around?

Hunter.

I scrunch my brow. What now? I start to type a response, but another text comes in.

He's blasting stuff all over Facebook about how he met Malik. They're not, like, BFFs now, are they?

I blow out a calming breath. It doesn't matter what Hunter's saying. We're not going to hang out with him, and he's not in my life.

Ugh, no. They met for a minute.

He's acting like they're totally bros or something.

I reply, Okay, but that's not that big of a deal, right?

WELLLLLL, she says.

My heart drops. Something is clearly up. I want to go to my laptop and look it up myself, but I can't. Why, oh why did I block him on Facebook?

Oh, right, because I didn't want to see pictures of him and Finley, that's why.

His friends were all impressed and Hunter was kind of soaking it up, and . . .

WHY IS SHE TYPING SO SLOWLY?

. . . He must've been trying to piece together how you met Malik, because I think he figured out Charles Buchannan lives at Sunrise House.

I swallow, then reply, It's not like he's going to show up and ask to meet Charles, right? And if he did, no one is going to let him in. We have protocols for crap like that.

Right? I mean, he can't do anything.

Except he found out you also live there.

WHO TOLD HIM??????

Oh crap. This is not good.

Brynn Michaels.

Rena's friend. So Alex clearly told Rena where I live, and Rena told Brynn.

Ugh. It's not like I was specifically keeping it a secret, but it also kind of never comes up. It was sort of lying by omission, not mentioning that, hey, I live in a retirement home. We just moved here in April.

But now, everyone I went to school with knows I live in a retirement home. And so does the third-richest person in the freakin' country. Oh god, what if people from school come over and, like, want to meet Malik? This *cannot* become some kind of circus. It could risk my mom's job.

So, uh, yeah, don't be surprised if Hunter shows up on your doorstop and tries to talk to you. Something tells me he wants an in with Malik.

I rub my face. Hunter . . . he just can't get in the middle of this. He's going to give me away to Malik.

What do I do?

I don't know.

I stare at my phone for a long second, pondering my options, when suddenly the text convo is replaced on the screen by an incoming call.

When I see the name, I freak out and toss the phone down on my bed. I step back. Hunter cannot be calling me.

After three rings, I regain my senses.

I can contain this. Like an oil spill. It's not lethal or anything. I just need to make it clear that I'm over him and want nothing to do with him. Or whatever. He'll move on.

I grab the phone and click Accept Call, bringing the phone to my ear as I try to calm my racing heart and level my voice. "Um, hello?"

"Holly," he says, and it sounds fake—way too sunny, like he's a cheerleader and not a football player.

I grip the phone harder. "Since when do you call me by my first name?"

"Don't be silly," he says, still sounding like he woke up on a rainbow. "We're on a first-name basis."

"But I don't *like* it," I snap. "I prefer you call me Mathews, like you always did."

Ugh, now I'm implying I want him to call me at all. Or like I'm . . . nostalgic. Gross.

"Okay, then, *Mathews*," he says, a little bit of the peppiness leaking from his voice. "Better?"

"Yes," I say. Because at least this way, if he *does* encounter me and Malik, he'll use my last name. "What's up?"

I grab the bottle of water off my nightstand, taking a swig.

"I thought we could hang out."

I choke and sputter out the water, slapping my chest and holding the phone away from my face. When I regain my composure, I rest the phone against my ear again. I knew he'd try to see Malik again, but I thought he'd at least be more subtle or beat around the bush or something. "Um, what?"

"Yeah, I thought maybe I could come over and we could chill."

"Come over here?"

"Yeah, to Sunrise House?"

"Hunter, we broke up."

"I know, but lots of people stay friends after breakups. I'm not trying to get back together or anything. I mean, you have a new boyfriend. Oh!" he says, his voice brightening again. "You know, to prove my intentions are pure, why not invite him over, too? You'll see I'm just being friendly."

I suppress a groan. "Not happening, Hunter."

"What?" He sounds so surprised, I almost believe it's genuine. "Why not?"

"I'm not stupid." Seriously, he thinks I'm this dense? That I can't see through his smarmy approach? I don't know what I ever saw in this guy.

"Of course you're not. I always trusted your calculus answers, didn't I?"

"Don't remind me," I grumble. I can't believe Alex never flicked me in the head and told me to open my eyes while I was dating this jerk.

"What?" he says.

I blow out a sigh. "Hunter, you just want to hang out with Malik."

There's a long pause, and I can tell he's battling the urge to deny it. "He seemed cool, okay? I think we have a lot in common."

"You don't even know him!"

"Yeah, but you do," he says. "I don't see why it's such a big deal."

"Because you're only doing this because of who he is."

The line goes quiet, and a million thoughts race through my head, solidifying into hope that he's going to back off and won't screw this up for me.

"Come on, Holiday . . ."

"Mathews," I correct. *Now* he starts calling me by my first name? Not when I was his girlfriend and was desperate to be treated as something other than one of the guys?

"Mathews," he says, sounding desperate. "Malik is a cool dude. You know he flew to the Super Bowl with the Seahawks?

Like, on the actual team plane. His grandpa is partial owner, and—"

If I don't get off the phone right now, I'm going to end up hurling it out the window.

"HUNTER. I'm serious. You're not going to just magically get a BFF who flies you around to exotic locations and introduces you to famous people and football players."

By his silence, I know I nailed it.

Wow, is this seriously the crap Malik deals with? I can't even imagine.

"Just think about it, okay? I really think he'd like me if we hung out."

"Good-bye, Hunter," I say, ending the call and going back to the text message box.

You're right, I type. We do have a problem. Call me when you're out of the car.

I toss my phone onto my bed and walk over to my photo collage, unpinning the few pictures Hunter is in. I grab a pair of blue-handled scissors from the cup on my desk and carefully trim him out, tossing the bits of photo paper right into the wicker trash can.

The pictures come out goofy—I have to cut off my arms where they wrap around his shoulders as we dance. But it's still an improvement. By the time I re-pin the last cropped photo, my phone rings.

"Hey," I say, tucking my phone between my shoulder and my ear.

"I swear that was the longest car ride ever," Alex replies. "I ran out of lives on Candy Crush, and my mom wouldn't let me turn the radio on."

I snort. "Do you need me to hashtag that 'first world problems' for you, or . . ."

She laughs. "Yeah, yeah. I know. So did you figure out what you're going to do about Hunter?"

"Avoid him at all costs?"

"Obviously."

"I told him we're not going to be friends, but I don't think it got through to him. So I think I'll make sure the front desk is clear that he's no guest of mine. I don't know what else to do."

"Good idea." There's something muffled in the background. "Dang, I gotta go. I'm standing outside a gas station and my mom's paying for her coffee already. Catch up later?"

"Yeah. Later."

I hang up the phone and glance down into my trash can, where Hunter's face stares back.

He better not ruin this for me.

CHAPTER NINETEEN

"Where are we going?" I ask Malik the following Sunday as we step out of his car. I glance up at the neon PIKE PLACE MARKET sign glowing a block away. "The market is closed." The summer air is cool against my bare legs as I follow him across the rough cobblestone road, my little heels sticking in the cracks, making me feel wobbly.

Or maybe it's because of the way Malik looks tonight. We're both a little dressier than normal, and the way his shirt hugs his shoulders, it's enough to send anyone off kilter.

"I have a key," he says, reaching over to hold my hand, as if to steady me on the uneven ground.

"You have a *key* to Pike Place," I respond, raising a brow.

He doesn't speak, just holds out a ring with a single key, swinging it in front of my nose. "Not to all the individual stores or anything, but to one of the side doors."

Wow. I shouldn't be surprised that he would have access to the biggest tourist destination in the city. After the Space Needle, I guess. Our movie-theater date proved he's got connections, but this . . . this is beyond.

He leads me around the corner, down an alley, and we pass the infamous gum wall—a wall a dozen feet wide and almost as high, stuck with chewed gum so thick you can no longer see the bricks. He unlocks a metal door, and we're in.

Pike Place after hours. It's almost eerie, how silent it is. Somewhere in the distance, a machine hums—a vacuum? An AC unit? But everything else is dark and shuttered. Strangely silent. Normally, a person can't go five feet in here without bumping elbows with another patron or without hearing the clink of change in a register, the music from the speakers, and the calling out of prices and specials.

Instead, it's just our footsteps echoing off the walls as he leads me down the long aisleway. We stop at a door emblazoned with a restaurant's name on the glass upper, but it's dark beyond.

"Um, pretty sure they're closed," I say, pointing at the door.

"I know," he says, pulling out the key ring again. Moments later, we're inside and he's flicking on lights.

"Are you sure this isn't going to get us in trouble?" I ask.

"Yes. My mom is friends with Tom Douglas. He gave me the key himself."

"Who?"

He narrows his eyes. "Tom Douglas?"

I shrug.

"You've lived in Seattle how long and you haven't dined at a Tom Douglas restaurant?"

"Um, no . . . ," I say, my voice trailing off. Crap. Tom Douglas must be some fancy chef or something. At someplace people like Malik have dined at a million times.

I glance over a menu left open near the front door. Dinners here cost fifty to sixty dollars. I try not to let my eyes flare wider—I'm supposedly used to dining like this—but I can't help it.

I guess the prices are beside the point anyway. Tom Douglas doesn't seem to be present.

"Huh," Malik says, studying me. Like having lived here without going to a Tom Douglas restaurant is a total crime. "I guess I'll have to take you to one. You don't know what you're missing."

"Sounds great," I say after a long moment, glancing back at the menu. "But this *is* Tom Douglas's restaurant, right?"

"Yes."

"But . . . he's obviously not around, so . . ."

"So, I hope you're hungry."

"You're cooking for me?" Surprise hits me full on, mixing with the heavy weight of guilt. This is a fling. He shouldn't be doing such thoughtful, romantic stuff.

"*We're* cooking for *us*," he corrects. "I thought it would be a fun activity to do together."

"Oh." *Fun.* Good. Flings are fun. Cooking together is fun. This is okay.

"What kind of 'oh' is that?" he asks, stopping. "We don't have to."

"No, it's a good oh," I say, blushing. "I love it. I'm just not a very good cook."

Moving into Sunrise House has been one of the best things ever, because I used to survive on PB and J or Easy-Mac cups I could microwave. Even though my mom usually worked on-site at whatever apartment complex we lived, she was working full-time and going to college at night, and I was often left to heat up microwave meals or order takeout.

"I took a culinary class at school," Malik says, interrupting my reminiscing. "So I'll share a few pointers."

I follow him toward the kitchen. His school has a culinary class? I mean, the public school I went to had home ec, but the fanciest thing we ever cooked were cupcakes, and mine always ended up caving in.

He hits a few switches inside the door, and two rows of fluorescent lights flicker to life. The kitchen is enormous, all stainless-steel surfaces and enormous, gleaming appliances.

Malik goes to the fridge, plucking out an armful of supplies, then turning and dumping them onto a counter.

I stay near the door, staring, taking in the way he navigates the kitchen with practiced ease. The way he knows where the knives are, the butter, everything.

He glances up, realizing I'm frozen in the doorway. "What?"

"Who else have you done this for?"

"What?"

"You're walking around here like you're used to cooking in this place," I say. "You've brought other girls here, haven't you?"

"What? No."

"Then why do you know where everything is?" I cross my arms, taking in his expression. He's got a sheepish smile, and his cheeks flush. "Wait . . . I've embarrassed you!"

"I've had this key for six months. I come here sometimes when I can't sleep. I've spent hours cooking here by myself. But no one knows. Other than the owner, obviously."

"Oh," I say, feeling guilty again.

"It's silly, because I have a kitchen at home, but I feel more comfortable in here. It's quiet and it feels right."

"Oh. Sorry. I didn't mean to accuse you."

"It's okay," he says, waving my concerns away. "Now, do you think you could wash the asparagus and trim off the stalky ends?" he asks. "I'll start on the chicken."

"Sure,'" I say, finally making my way around the expanse of countertops. He grabs a white apron off a nearby hook, and I allow him to lift it over my head and pull my hair out of the way. The maneuver feels oddly intimate, his fingers sliding across the skin at the back of my neck so softly and deliberately that I find myself holding my breath.

He ties the strings and turns away.

I reach for the asparagus, determined to work and not stare at him, but it's impossible.

His sleeves are rolled up, and he's wearing his own apron, looking more like an executive chef than a teenager. With each practiced slice and casual dash of salt or drizzle of vinegar, he looks more and more like he belongs here.

"Let me guess," I say, after I'm done trimming the asparagus. "Your grandpa also doesn't know you love cooking?"

His knife slips, and he narrowly misses slicing into his fingers. "What?"

"You. This," I say, waving my hand around. "The fact that you come here to cook at night, when they're closed, instead of doing it at home. He doesn't know, does he?"

"Oh."

"Plus, most guys pick shop class or leadership as an elective. You picked cooking."

"Maybe I was just hoping to impress my future girlfriend," he says, flashing me a cocky smile. But I see through it. The longer I know Malik, the more I realize that the person he presents and the face he puts on are not who he really is. "By cooking her a five-star dinner at one of the most exclusive restaurants in the city."

I turn to him, leaning a hip against the counter. "Or maybe you're afraid to be yourself."

He slides the knife out of the way, reaching for a pan and drizzling it with oil. "I'm being myself *now*, aren't I?"

"But you hide your talents and interests from your own grandfather?"

"I'm not hiding," he says. "But it's not like I can walk in here and cook like this when the restaurant is open. I'd be in the way."

"I just mean . . . I don't think your grandfather is trying to be judgmental. I just don't think he *knows* you. You grew up two states away. Maybe if you trusted him to accept you, really showed him who you are *now*, he'd learn to trust you. Realize you're not that boy who crashes cars in the Hollywood Hills anymore, you know?"

He stares at the pan. "Yeah. I know. I'm getting that, with your help. But it doesn't happen overnight, okay?"

"I wonder what it's like," I say as he finally moves again, sliding the pan over a little so it's centered on the blue flame.

He rubs the back of his neck with his free hand. "What?"

"Assuming the worst all the time. Being so afraid to be yourself."

He sighs deeply. "Look, I know you have a point. I know he sees me as who I used to be, and I need to change that," he says, turning away to go to the fridge.

I lean my hip against the counter. "Next time you're at his place, let him see a new side of you. Cook him lunch. Not a sandwich. Something . . . impressive."

He closes the fridge, meeting my eyes. "Fine. I'll do it."

CHAPTER TWENTY

The next morning, I pull up at Alex's house, gliding to a stop behind Rena's sporty red coupe. I put the car in park and stare for a long minute, trying to focus.

It's impossible. I barely slept last night, in spite of the fact that I should've been exhausted by the time I slipped into bed at two a.m., full of the most delicious food in the history of the universe.

I can't stop thinking about how close we're getting. How he's showing me more and more of himself, and it's *wrong* to keep doing this, to keep lying.

I'm not just lying to him. I'm lying to myself. This feels like more than a fling. This feels . . . important.

Grabbing the paper handles of two craft-shop bags, I lock my crappy car and cross the lawn. Last night, Malik dropped me off on the porch, and I had to slip inside and wait until I heard his car pull away before I could jog across the street to my own car and go home.

Thank god Alex's parents weren't awake. That would've been awkward.

At the door, I head in without waiting for an answer to my halfhearted knock. I've been hanging out here so long, I hardly need to get permission. But these days, the only time I'm over here is when I'm pretending the house is mine.

I blink, the full impact of that hitting me. Alex barely ever invites me over anymore. I'm only here today because I suggested it, wanting to fill Alex in on all the gory details of my date. Also, I'm hoping she can convince me I am not a terrible person for what I'm doing.

And, of course, Rena is here. Ugh.

Rena's and Alex's raucous laughter trickles downstairs to greet me, and I take the steps two by two. The last one creaks under my feet, and the laughter dies off abruptly. By the time I get to her room, I feel like I'm party crashing or something, because they're silent, both looking at me as I step into the doorway.

"Um, hey," I say dumbly. "I, uh, brought the beads."

"Cool," Alex says brightly, jumping up off her bed. She glances back at Rena, but I can't see her expression. I swallow, ignoring the hollow feeling at the base of my throat.

The feeling that says when I suggested we get together, she agreed out of obligation.

"I was telling Rena about how you do that cool thing with interweaving the beads, and I thought you could show us how to do it."

That can't be what they were talking about, because my methods are in no way hilarious and entertaining.

"Um, yeah, sure," I say, walking to her desk and setting the shopping bags down. I arrange the little plastic bags in a line, the big chunky beads on one end and the sparkly colored beads on the other. "Um, I got us each a blown-glass one too, with our initials," I say, grabbing the *A* and the *R* and holding them out.

"Oh," Rena says, lighting up. "I just got the *best* idea." She plucks one of the little bags out of my hand. "I'll do yours, and you do mine, okay?" Rena says, tossing the *R* bead over to Alex, who grabs and misses.

"Done," she says, scooping the bag off the floor.

My lips part, and I want to point out that there's no one for me to trade with, but I resist, snapping my mouth shut again.

I'm being stupid. Overly sensitive. They're probably just oblivious to how left out I always feel.

Or maybe they're just being jerks.

I grab a bundle of stretchy cord, unwinding it. "Hold your wrist out," I say, motioning to Rena, who obediently complies. I measure out a length of thread, then snip it off. "You too."

After they both have the right length of cord, I open my plastic case and dump the beads I purchased today into the available empty slots. Then I turn around and demonstrate the new trick Alex was talking about, how I can double-back periodically on the thread, creating a bracelet that looks more like it belongs in a jewelry store and less like it was made by a child.

The room falls silent as we slide on the first few beads, and then Alex reaches over and flips on the radio.

An old Fergie song hums through the speakers.

"Oh my god, I love this song!" Rena tosses her barely started bracelet aside and jumps up onto Alex's bed, belting out about how she's glamorous.

I glance over at Alex, expecting her to roll her eyes or at least tell Rena to get off her bed, but she's already jumping up beside her. And when the Ludacris part comes in, she does a surprisingly intense lip-syncing version that sends Rena off into hysterics.

I feel like a voyeur. Like I'm on the outside looking in, completely separate from them.

This was stupid. I never should've come over. I knew something was off with my friendship with Alex, and it's clear now that whatever connection she has with Rena has caused her to completely replace me as her best friend.

I stare at them for a few bars of the song, wondering when Alex loosened up like this. I was always the offbeat one, the one who didn't mind being silly. Alex's mom used to scold me for doing stuff like jumping out of the closet at Alex and making her scream.

I turn back to my bracelet and focus, *really hard*, on finding the perfect beads. The song transitions, switching to a soft-rock one I don't recognize, and Rena and Alex burst into laughter.

Startled, I glance up, and Rena's falling against Alex, laughing so hard, she apparently can't hold up her own body.

"Oh my god, do you remember—"

"That weird guy at the gas station—"

"And he was all—"

"You really do have eyes like the stars," they say simultaneously, and then laugh harder, until Alex flops down on her own bed, and I'm pretty sure she's about to die of asphyxiation. Meanwhile, Rena is clutching her sides, doubled over.

Alex finally sees me staring and sits up, her chest heaving as she struggles to regain her breath. "Sorry, we heard this song at a gas station a few weeks ago, and this *totally* skeevy guy was hitting on Rena," she says.

"Oh," I say, failing to laugh. This is . . . awkward.

"I guess it's one of those you-had-to-be-there kind of things," Rena adds. "But trust me, it was hilarious. He had the world's dumbest mustache."

"I see," I say, even though I don't. Even though I want to know why I wasn't there, why Alex didn't tell me this supposedly super-hilarious story before now.

But I know the answer to that question.

Alex has left me behind.

An hour later, I'm ready to leave. It's too draining, pretending I don't notice that I'm sitting a foot too far away to be really part of things. Pretend I can't see as clear as day that while Alex might be my best friend, I'm no longer hers.

The longer I sit here, the more it hurts. One more minute and my heart is going to shatter into a million pieces.

I abruptly pick up my phone, as if a text came in even though it didn't. Even though my phone isn't even on silent. "Oh, shoot. I forgot I told my mom I'd help her out tonight," I lie.

"Aw, really?" Alex asks. "I thought maybe we could go watch that new J-Law movie."

"You remembered?" I ask, the oddest sense of relief overcoming me. So she hasn't totally forgotten about me. It was the last one we agreed to watch. A theater trailer that we'd picked out together.

"Of course," she says, like I am being silly. "*Tradition?*"

"It's super-good," Rena agrees. "You'll love it. We both freaked out at the end."

I pause, and the relief fizzles, hollowing me out. "Wait, you've already seen it?"

"Yeah, but we can totally go see it again," Alex says. She's not very apologetic. It's like she doesn't even get it. "It's honestly *that* good."

"Oh. Um, no, that's okay," I say, standing, turning away so she can't see that she's hurt me. "I really do have to go help my mom."

I snap the cases shut and shove them into the paper bags, and then I turn toward the door, still avoiding her gaze. "Have fun though, guys. See you around."

I don't wait for their responses before I rush out the door, blinking back the tears.

Alex and I are still friends, but we're not best friends.

And in a few more weeks, there's going to be a full state between us, and maybe the first part won't even be true anymore.

CHAPTER TWENTY-ONE

I'm on a mission.

If Malik is going to show me who *he* really is, then it's time he sees how I live. And date. The idea of it kind of freaks me out—this date is the closest thing to *real* I've shown him. But I can't help it.

And so, barely a week after he took me here, I'm taking him back. I'm gripping his hand, dragging him toward Pike Place. Today, he's going to see it the way everyone else sees it: crowded and raucous and pulsing with life.

"Where are you taking me, exactly?"

"On a real date," I say, dragging him through the crowd packing the sidewalk.

"We've been on dates," he says, struggling to keep up with me, turning his shoulders sideways to slip past a huge guy in a ball cap. "Were those not real enough for you?" He drags me to a stop when I step onto the uneven brick road. Ahead, the iconic neon sign greets us, mounted high over the building. There are fruit stands lining the street, and a slow march of cars fights its way through the narrow, alleylike road.

The building itself looks simple, sprawling in both directions and open where it faces the street. But it's deceptively large, an eclectic labyrinth of levels and twisting halls, each floor filled with windup-toy stores and record shops and antiques and fresh fruit.

"Wait, are we going back to Pike Place Market?"

"Yes."

He furrows his brow. "How is it a real date if you take me here, but not if I take you?"

"Those dates were about who *you* are. It's my turn to show you who *I* am."

"Oh," he says as we stop next to a huge bronze pig statue.

"This is where we start," I say, digging into my pocket and handing him a five-dollar bill and a quarter.

"And . . . what am I doing with these?" he asks.

"We're going to walk through the market. Every time we come to a turn or a staircase, we flip the coin to decide which way to go."

He holds up the bill. "That explains the quarter, but the five dollars?"

I pull out a scrap of paper and hand it over.

He reads aloud, "'Something sweet, something from the sea, something colorful, something to hang on a wall, and something to wear.'" He furrows his brow and looks up at me. "What's this?"

"The first person to buy items that hit all five of those points wins."

He furrows his brow. "But you only gave me five dollars."

"Hmm," I say, playfully punching him in the shoulder. "I guess you'll have to be creative. Or a good bargainer."

"I'm supposed to cover the whole list with five dollars?"

"Yep."

By the look on his face, it's pretty clear he's never had a budget before, and it's all I can do to hold in my laughter.

"Okaaaaay, then," he says, the challenge setting in. "And when I succeed, what do I win?"

I grin widely. "That's for me to know and for you to find out. Just trust me . . . you don't want to be the loser."

He bites his lower lip. "Um, okay."

"But you can't cheat. Once one of us buys an item from a booth, that booth is officially off-limits—for both of us. So if I find an item from the list, you can't just copy me and buy the same thing. You have to go somewhere new."

I see the look in his eyes and I know he's in. Intrigue. Curiosity. Excitement. "Okay. Deal. Let's do it."

"Okay, then. Flip the coin. Heads we go right; tails we go left."

Malik tosses the coin into the air, then catches it and flips it over on the top of his hand. "Left."

We walk under the roofline of the market and swing left, passing where tourists watch men throw fish. There's a huge crowd of people, cell phones held up to snap pictures of the fish the moment it flies through the air, so I can't quite see the booth . . . only the giant bays of ice and seafood.

Malik pauses, surveying a flower stall, his eyes roaming the prices.

They're five to ten dollars per bouquet. A moment later, he shrugs and moves away from the stall.

Instead of following, I walk to the woman stooped over in front of the booth, trimming the bottom of a bouquet before dropping it back into the bucket of water.

"Hey, is there any way I could get just three stems? Baby's breath or something would be fine."

The woman glances up, then around her stall, and points at a black plastic vase of pink carnations. "Would those work?"

"For a dollar, they would."

A second later, she's handing me three stems and I'm pocketing the four dollars of change.

"Something colorful?" Malik says.

"Give me a second." I start with the longest stem, twisting it around the second longest before I pull in the other and curl it around to create a loop.

I plop it on top of my head and grin at Malik. "Something colorful *and* something to wear."

"I think I may have underestimated you," he says, studying me with an appraising expression.

"I think perhaps you're right. And you're going to regret that."

We continue past the stall, but Malik abruptly doubles back to the seafood one we'd passed at the entrance. I follow.

A moment later, he has purchased precisely one oyster. "Something from the sea," he says, holding it up. "I don't suppose I could argue that it could go on the wall?"

I snicker. "No."

We head down the aisle again until a stairwell appears beside us.

"Heads we go straight, tails we go down the steps."

Malik tosses the coin again, and we find ourselves descending farther into the market, to where the floors creek and the ceilings are a bit lower.

A few steps into the hall, Malik grabs my hand, tugging me into a photo booth. I raise a brow at him but don't comment as he feeds three dollars into the booth.

That means he'll only have one dollar left.

He puts his arm around me and we lean in, cheek-to-cheek, as the first flash goes off. For the second, he turns, kissing my temple as I stare at the camera.

"Funny face," I say, sticking my tongue out to the side and widening my eyes as much as possible. Malik is thrown for a second and is halfway to a funny face when the flash goes off. I laugh so hard, I can't pose for the next one before the fourth and final flash hits.

"Don't tell me you've never done a funny face in a photo booth," I say.

"Um, I've totally done funny faces in a photo booth?"

I roll my eyes and slide out of the booth. "Wow, you really grew up in your own little bubble, huh?"

We stand outside the booth, waiting for the strip to slide out. "I guess you could say that."

The photo drops into the slot, and he holds it up.

"Something to hang on the wall?"

He nods. "Plus, *you're* in the picture, so . . ."

"So what?"

"Something sweet."

I can't help the grin that overtakes my face. "You're a cheese-ball."

He steps in, wrapping his arms around my shoulders and squeezing me close. I lean against him, enjoying his embrace before stepping back.

"But that doesn't mean I'm going to let you win."

"Pull in here," I direct Malik two hours later. I point to the Chevron station coming up on our right and lean down to grab my purse off the floorboard.

He's clearly decided to sit back and see where the night takes us because he obediently pulls into the station, stopping against the curb and putting the car in park.

"I'll be right back."

I dash into the store, spend another five dollars, and when I come back out, I toss my purse back onto the floorboard of Malik's car. It's only then that I wonder if my next move will damage his car in any way, but it's too late to pull back.

"Um, pop the trunk, I guess."

When he sees me open up the block ice chest near the door to the station and pull out two blocks, he gets out and takes them from my hands, tossing them into the trunk of his hundred-thousand-dollar car as if it totally doesn't matter if we drive around town with them melting in the back.

"That way," I say, pointing to the right as we pull out.

Five minutes later, we're pulling into Gasworks Park.

We climb out and get the ice, then walk to a grassy knoll not far from the car.

"So . . . are we opening a shaved ice stand, or . . . ?"

I grin triumphantly, and his expression slides from teasing to concern.

"Um, why am I suddenly worried?" he asks.

"Set the ice there," I say, and point to the very peak of the hill.

When he does, I rip into the bag, setting the block near the edge of the slope. Then I use the bag itself to cover the top of the ice. "Okay, there you go. Climb aboard."

He stares at me. "You want me to sit on a block of ice."

"Yep. You shouldn't get your pants wet or anything. The plastic will protect you."

"And what do you suppose I do then?"

"Ride it."

He narrows his eyes, glancing between the block and the hill. "You want me to do what?"

"It's like sledding. But a summer version."

He gapes at the block of ice as if it's a UFO. "There's no way that's a thing."

"Oh, it's a thing. Trust me on that." I grin.

"Are you sure this isn't going to kill me?"

I tip my head to the side, popping my hand on my hip. "Are you sure you're not averse to having fun?"

"Oh, I'm fine with a little fun," he says, glancing up from the ice block. "But I'm talking roller coasters. Jet Skiing. Snowboarding. But this . . ."

"Oh, come on," I tease. "Live a little."

"You've done this?"

I nod. "Yes. And I'm going to today, too. That's why we have two blocks of ice. But you lost, which means you have to go first."

"Oh."

"It's not going to kill you. You can trust me. It's fun."

"Then why is it a punishment for the loser?"

"Because it's more terrifying if you've never seen anyone else do it first," I say, grinning wider. I love that he's so thrown. So out of his comfort zone.

There's something very gratifying about a guy who practically owns the world looking so uncomfortable in it.

His jaw drops. "You set me up! You knew I'd lose. And if I didn't, it's not much of a punishment for you, is it?"

I bite my lower lip and look away, trying to fight a smile or find a way to deny what he's saying, but I can't. Because, yes, today was about messing with him, pushing him, forcing him to see the world through someone else's eyes.

He walks over and wraps his arms around me, spinning me in a playful circle. "I'll forgive you," he says, "but we do this together."

"I don't know, you kind of agreed."

"And you kind of tricked me," he says. "So, can we call it even?"

"Fine, crybaby," I say, stooping down to rip open the bag on the other block of ice. I position it a couple of feet from his, both blocks sitting lengthwise. "Just to warn you, though . . . it's kind of hard to steer."

"Kind of?"

"Like maybe impossible. You just gotta be okay with the fact that you're going to crash at some point."

He frowns, staring down at the block. "Did you grow up around here? I feel like this is from, like, *Honey Boo Boo* or something."

"It's not from some redneck show. It's just what high school people do when they have too much time on their hands and not *your* kind of budget. Sit on the ice."

"Four words I never thought I'd hear from my girlfriend," he jokes, following my instructions.

I sit down beside him, straddling the block of ice and belatedly remembering just how fast the chill seeps through a pair of jeans. "Okay, ready?"

"I was born ready," he says.

I raise a brow. "I bet the only time you've been sledding was in, like, Vail or Whistler or something. Probably using sleds plated in gold."

"They were plastic."

"Was it Vail or Whistler?"

I know he wants to deny it, but he just shakes his head. "Vail."

"Yeah. So, anyway, *this* is different."

"Okay, then," he says, taking a deep breath. By his expression you'd think he just jumped on a bull, not a block of ice. "I'm ready."

"Right. One," I say, my heart rate spiking. "Two . . ."

"Three," he says, and we shove off.

The first moment is always the worst. As we crest the edge of the hill, a dozen thoughts run through my mind, including that this might be the biggest hill in the history of the universe. But mostly that we might die and everyone in this entire country will blame me for killing the richest, most attractive boy I've ever met.

Then the blocks steady out, and relief whooshes through me as we pick up speed.

"Holy . . . ," he says.

I think I'm screaming or shrieking or laughing or some weird combination of all three as we hit the halfway point, the wind whistling past our ears. If he says anything after that, it's impossible to hear.

We slide over a small knoll halfway down the main slope, and it throws off my balance. I reach out to grab him, but his ice has angled away, the gap between us widening.

Then he's going down backward as his block spins around and slides back in my direction, colliding with mine.

We tip off our blocks, his body tumbling down the hill over mine, until all our limbs are intertwined. He lands on top of me, his elbows propped up to keep from crushing me.

I giggle, staring up into his eyes, taking in the sparkle there . . . the life.

"That . . . was . . . amazing," he says. "And terrifying. Let's never do it again."

I laugh and am about to wiggle out from under him when he leans down, brushing his lips against mine.

At that very moment, I know I'm in love with him.

CHAPTER TWENTY-TWO

"You are not going to believe this!" Alex screams into my ear.

I yank my phone away, my ear ringing, and blink. I've been on the couch for the last two hours, staring at the ceiling and daydreaming about Malik. Daydreaming about him has practically become my full-time job. I must have zonked out or something because the ringing phone, and then Alex's scream, just brought me back into the real world.

"Uh, Holly?" her voice sounds tinny with the phone removed from my ear.

"Sorry," I say, putting the phone back up to my ear. "I thought maybe my brain exploded from the frequency with which you just screamed. Um, what am I not going to believe?"

"My mom will kill me if I try to come over because she's been cooking all evening. You know, slaving away all day over a hot stove, blah blah blah, guilt trip, guilt trip. So get over here right now and I'll show you. I want to see your face when you see it."

"Um, what are you showing me?"

"Just get here now. I promise it will be worth it."

She immediately hangs up like she knows I can't resist the mystery. Which I can't. I groan and sit up, wondering if the couch cushions have a Holly-shaped indent in them yet, and go to find my keys.

Fifteen minutes later, I pull to a stop at the curb. I'm reaching toward the passenger side floorboard to grab my purse when something slams into my window, and I jump so hard my seatbelt—still buckled—bites into my neck.

Alex is standing just outside my door, pressing something against the window. I open my mouth to yell at her for startling me, but then I look at what she's holding against the glass.

US Weekly.

It's the same feature I saw Malik in two weeks in, that stupid "Stars: They're Just Like Us" one. Except this time, he's at the mall, his arm slung over a girl's shoulder as he beams at her, and she's smiling back.

Holy moly.

It's me.

"Let me see that up close," I say, clicking Alex's bedroom door shut. My heart is thudding in my chest so hard, I can barely breathe. I'm in a magazine. I don't even know how they got this picture. It's not like that lady at the mall looked like a professional—she was using her cell phone. I certainly didn't see flashes or paparazzi or whatever. Aren't they supposed to be obvious? Big groups of guys with giant lenses on their cameras, shouting people's names?

"Get your own," she says, waving her hand at me to keep me at bay.

My jaw drops. "Alex! Obviously, I didn't buy one, considering I didn't know I was in it!"

She reaches over to her desk, yanking open the drawer with a big screech and pulling out another magazine. She flings it in my direction, her eyes still trained on the page.

"You bought more than one?"

"My best friend is in it! Of course I did."

For a second I hardly move. *My best friend.* She still considers me her best friend.

I realize she's staring at me, clearly waiting for me to take a closer look at the picture So I flip to the page, but before I can read the tiny text on the side, Alex does for me.

"Malik Buchannan and a mysterious, dark-haired girl cruise a Seattle shopping mall. Who is the lucky girl?"

"This is stupid," I say, my finger gliding across the glossy page. "Who even gives a crap about him hanging out with me? This isn't even a story."

"These magazines have to create stories out of thin air. It's what they do."

"Since when are you TMZ's biggest fan?"

"You can't be that surprised. Golden boy dropped off the radar for months, and people figured he was settling down or decided to become a monk or something. And then *bam*, they find him in Seattle, and you're with him? It's totally a story."

"Ugh, it shouldn't be."

"Oh, come on, you're with the richest dude under thirty in this entire country, and he's freaking hot to boot. Of course people are obsessed. Now you're a part of that."

"So what do I do?"

"Frame it?"

I roll my eyes. "This is bad. If people do some digging, they're going to find out my name. And then *Malik* will find out the truth, and the summer fling he's supposed to think back on with fond memories is going to seem more like a nightmare. He *trusts* me, Alex."

Her eyes widen, and she glances between me and the magazine again, as if picturing the headline. "Oh. Crap. You're right." She plunks down in her desk chair. "I totally did not think of that. Um, yikes?"

"Yes, yikes!"

"Maybe you two just need to keep things on the down low. Casual dates."

"I kind of thought hanging out at Pike Place Market qualified as casual. We spent a total of ten dollars and were in a big crowd of *normal* people."

"I meant, like, in less public places, you know? Although I guess I didn't really expect paparazzi to be hitting up the market, either. Maybe it's not even paparazzi. Maybe regular people sent them this picture. Everyone has cameras, so . . ."

"Exactly! And if we can't even go somewhere as simple as the market, what do we do? It's not like I can invite him over for a movie!" I pause, the full implication of my lie hitting me. "Hi, Malik, I'm not at all the girl you thought I was—I didn't even tell you my real name! Check out this fantastic tiny little apartment we can hang out in! It just happens to be inside the retirement home where your grandfather lives! Isn't it just your dream come true?"

"Whoa, calm down," Alex says, pursing her lips and trying not to laugh.

"Well, I have to do something. Or I'm going to end up as some fabled mystery girl in every issue of this freaking magazine until they figure out who I am, and then it's all over."

"I'm sure there are other options." She screws her lips to the side, deep in thought. "What about the drive-in? As long as you stay inside the car, no one would even notice he's there. Plus, steamy make-out sessions."

"His car does *not* blend in. And I can't keep using yours for everything. You don't even have tinted windows. And what if he needed to go use a restroom or wanted snacks? It's a no-go."

"Okay, so why not just go to his house?" Alex spins her desk chair around, propping her feet up on the desk and crossing them at the ankles. I don't know how she can be so casual about this.

"We do," I say, slapping the magazine shut and sliding it away from me. "But it's not like I can invite myself over there all the time. People do that, you know. They're curious what it looks like and really just want to come over for a tour. He'll think I'm one of those people if I just keep saying I want to go to his place."

"Okay, um, you could go do something with his grandpa. Use Sunrise House as your cover. There's no way paparazzi hang out at that place."

"They might, if they figure out Charles Buchannan lives there. And besides, I'm supposed to stay away from him. And everyone at Sunrise House knows my name is Holly. I managed to come up with a cover story about loving holidays, but it'll fall apart eventually."

"Huh."

"Yeah." I sigh, flopping down on her bed, staring up at the funky sticker jewels Alex and I stuck up there on the ceiling in the ninth grade. "I don't know. Maybe I should just end it now. Before he finds out the truth."

"You're really going to stick with the plan? You're going to end it when you go away to college?"

"Yes. I think. Just thinking about it fills me with dread. But if he finds out I've been lying all this time, it could totally set him back. He has a hard time trusting people as it is." I blow out another a sigh. "And he ditched people in the past, when he realized they had ulterior motives for being around him."

"You don't have ulterior motives, though," she points out. "It's just a misunderstanding."

"I know, but does it matter? It's still lying." I frown. "I don't deserve a guy like him."

Alex stares at me, like she's reading between everything I said. "Oh my god, you're totally falling for him, aren't you?"

"What?" I said, shaking my head vehemently. "That's ridiculous. We just met, like, five or six weeks ago."

But her expression doesn't change. She just keeps staring at me, a knowing smile playing at her lips. "You didn't answer the question."

Because I'm not ready to say it aloud. I'm not ready to openly acknowledge the truth.

I furrow my brow. "He's amazing, okay? Completely and totally amazing and unlike anyone I've ever met."

"Okay, then. What you need to do is to wait for him to be in love with you. Wait for him to see you for who you really are. And then when you tell him, he'll know you had the right intentions and will forgive you. And then you won't have to break up with him."

I study the spot on the ceiling where the fading sunlight reflects off the biggest fake jewel sticker, a bright pink one in the center. "*Or* waiting for him to fall for me just means I will really, really hurt him when he learns the truth."

"I mean, I know you—you would never in a million years intentionally lie or hurt *anyone*. He'll see that. He'll know you didn't mean for this to happen. And then you can explain why you did it, and he'll get it. He'll be able to see that it wasn't malicious."

"I guess that's not a bad plan," I say, warming up to the idea that maybe this thing doesn't have to be a fling. That maybe I can tell him the truth and he won't find my tiny lie such a big deal. That he won't think I'm just like everyone else in his life.

"It's a fantastic plan," Alex says, her voice laced with satisfaction, as if she just solved world hunger. "So . . . can I, like, frame this?"

I pick up the pillow on her bed and hurl it at her face.

CHAPTER TWENTY-THREE

Twenty minutes later, I'm standing on the porch at Alex's house, her car key in one hand and my phone in the other, pressed to my ear.

When Malik picks up, it's all I can do to keep my heart from doing a silly little jig. "Hey, you," he says.

"Hey. Want to hang out?"

"Sure," he says. "I just got home from the office, but I can come over."

"I'm not at home," I say. At least it's not a lie. "I'm closer to your house than mine. I can swing by, and then maybe we can decide what to do with ourselves?"

"Sounds great."

"Cool. See you then."

I hang up the phone, then turn around and open the front door, sticking my head in. "I'll have it back in a few hours, okay?" I holler up the stairs.

"Sure, whatever!" Alex says.

"Thanks!"

In my eagerness to see Malik, I slam the door a little too hard. Then I dash across the lawn and slip into the driver's seat of Alex's car.

He must've told the guard I was coming, because I don't even come to a full stop at the gatehouse before the guy waves, and the gate opens.

I park next to a big fountain, which is currently spraying a dozen feet or so into the air, and climb out of Alex's car. I go to lock it, then realize I'm being silly. It's parked behind a fortress of a wall, with an actual guard.

I walk past two men in green EMERALD CITY LANDSCAPING T-shirts. They're trimming a pair of potted bushes that sit on either side of the front entry into little spirals.

I approach the front door and am just raising my fist to knock when it swings open.

Malik stands in the frame, looking the most casual I've ever seen him, in a crisp blue T-shirt and khaki shorts, his feet bare.

Something about those bare feet makes my heart rate spike.

"Hey," he says, stepping forward to hug me.

"Hi," I say, suddenly oddly shy.

"Come on in," he says. I kick off my shoes, just to put us on level terms. The marble in the entry is cool against the soles of my feet. But being barefoot in this place somehow puts me more at ease.

It makes it feel more like a home and less like a gallery or something.

I glance over at the grand staircase with its carved teak spindles. "So, do I get to see your bedroom this time?" I ask. "You've seen mine, after all."

It's a lie, of course, but as I say it, I realize I wish I could show him my *real* room. I can't help but wonder if he's drawn any conclusions about me based on Alex's room. Pictured me on a soccer team or showing a dog in 4-H, or whatever.

Or maybe he just thinks I have an obsession with large birds that may or may not look like pterodactyls.

"Um, sure, I guess," he says, but there's hesitation to his voice.

Intriguing. Maybe there's a reason we stayed on the ground floor that day we were looking for antiques.

"I should know what my boyfriend's bedroom looks like, after all," I say, poking him in the side. "I'm picturing . . . a big Seahawks banner."

He shakes his head. "I'm not into sports."

"But you flew with the te—"

I stop myself, just as he freezes and stares, one hand on the railing. There's an emotion in his eyes I've never seen before. That I never want to see again. "What did you do," he grinds out, "Google me?"

"What?" I say too quickly. "No."

But he's still not moving. "How did you know I went to the Super Bowl? I didn't tell you that."

Fear. That's what his expression is. A mixture of fear and disappointment.

It's exactly how he'll look at me if he learns about my lies.

"Hunter called me," I say, cringing. "I didn't want to mention it because he's not really worth it. But he's basically convinced you two are a bromance waiting to happen." The scary look fades, and Malik rolls his eyes. "He kind of let it slip about the team plane. I told him to unpack his bags, that I'm not hooking him up with a new bff."

"Ah." More of the tension dissipates in his shoulders, and he turns back to the staircase, his hand sliding along the railing.

"Wait," I say, climbing a few steps, so that I'm standing one higher than he is and can look him directly in the eyes. "It's there, isn't it?"

"What?"

"The doubts," I say. "About me. About whether I'm genuine. They're there, in the back of your mind. You think you're going to find out I'm after you for who you are. For . . . this," I say, circling my finger around in the air, motioning to the house.

"Maybe." He chews on his lip, glancing down at our feet.

"Hey," I say softly.

He glances up again.

"I don't care about this." I gesture to the ceiling, where a chandelier draped in crystals hangs. "I care about *you*."

"Yeah, I know," he says softly. "But that doesn't mean it's easy to silence the doubts." He reaches out, rubbing his thumb in little circles on my cheek. I hold my breath, soaking in the warmth of his skin against mine, and then we turn and head up the stairs together, side by side.

"Okay, so no sports memorabilia," I say, changing the subject, eager to leave the heaviness behind. "So . . . band posters?"

"No. Definitely not."

"Not into music?"

He shrugs. "Not enough to hang posters."

Before I can come up with any other ideas, he's pushing open a big six-paneled oak door and we're stepping into an enormous bedroom bathed in natural light. In the center of the room is the biggest four-poster bed I've ever seen, with a navy comforter and a pile of pillows.

But that's not what takes my breath away.

It's the books.

Books are everywhere.

Downstairs, in his grandfather's study . . . library . . . the shelves were filled with books, but in an orderly, beautiful way. The books were almost uniform, their leather spines lined up perfectly.

This is like an explosion. There's a small, haphazard stack on the nightstand next to his bed. But it's the shelves along every wall practically bursting with books stacked in different directions that capture my attention.

"This is beautiful," I say, walking to the closest shelf, letting my fingers trail over the cracked spines. Also unlike the library downstairs, these books aren't leather bound. They're not even hardback. They're mass market paperbacks, worn out like they could be folded and tucked into Malik's pocket.

"Did you bring all these up from California?"

"Most of them. I'm sure the moving company loved it."

I move along the shelves, studying the titles.

"That wall is science fiction," he says, "and the other two are fantasy."

"You really are a nerd," I tease, but when I glance back at him, his cheeks really are flushed. "Wait, are you embarrassed by this?"

He steps up beside me, running his hand across the spines of the nearest book. "Maybe a little."

"That's silly."

"Is it?"

"Of course. You need to quit being embarrassed by things you love."

He shrugs. "My grandpa wouldn't get it."

I cross my arms. "I think the hang-up is *yours*," I say. "I think you're afraid to be yourself around him."

He frowns. "Maybe that's true."

"You need to start showing him who you are. Your passions. I think he'll surprise you." I glance out the window, at the way the sun is glimmering off the lake. "Let's get out of this house."

"That's abrupt."

"We're getting too serious," I say, playfully punching his shoulder. "We need air."

"Okay. I know just the place."

CHAPTER TWENTY-FOUR

It's not until Malik and I slip our shoes off, and my toes sink into the sand at Alki Beach, that I wonder why I've never come down here.

It's one of the few sandy beaches in Seattle, surrounded by million-dollar homes with spectacular views. The gentle waves of Puget Sound lap against the edges of the shore, and seagulls squawk as they fly overhead.

It's breezier than I expected. As I shiver, Malik slides off his jacket and puts it around my shoulders.

"It's pretty here," I say, taking in the shoreline. "Busier than I expected."

That much is true. There are people everywhere—on beach towels, picnic tables, and even playing volleyball. I didn't expect crowds like this. I can't help but dart a glance around, wondering if the people fiddling with their phones are secretly videotaping us or snapping our pictures.

If they are, Malik is oblivious.

"Do you come here often?" I cringe as the words leave my mouth. "Sorry. That sounds lame."

He laughs. "Not really. I thought you'd like it, though."

"Yeah? Do I scream sandy beaches to you?"

He spins around, making a fake photo frame with his fingers. "Yeah, I'm seeing it now. You, Venice Beach, roller blades . . ."

"I've never been to California."

He drops his hands. "Really? Why not? It's hardly more than a two-hour flight to LA."

"Um . . ." My voice trails off. I'm tired of lying. "I've never actually been on a flight at all."

"Seriously?"

I nod, anxiety tightening in my chest as the first real truth slips loose. "Yeah."

"Afraid?"

I shake my head. "Um, no, it's not that." The words bubble up in my throat. "We, um, haven't always been as well off as we are now."

He reaches out for my hands, and I interlace my fingers with his, allowing him to pull us toward where the waves meet the sand. The water is cool against first my toes, then my ankles, before he stops. The glare of the sun on the water makes him squint, casting shadows over his eyes.

For a long moment, I worry I've screwed up. That this thread of honesty will open the floodgates between us, that he'll ask probing questions and realize there are way, *way* more things I've kept hidden.

But he glances over at me, and the setting sun glints off his teeth as he flashes me a smile.

"I'll bring you down to LA sometime. The beaches are so different. Huntington is my favorite."

"Yeah? Why?"

"It's . . . more pure. The quietest. Just the sand and the waves, really, but it's got some of the best restaurants in the area. Venice has the busy boardwalk and gym and shops, and Santa Monica's got the big pier. Huntington is just . . . the beach, and I like the unobstructed beauty of it."

"What about Disneyland?" I ask.

"Huh?"

"What's it like?"

"You want to know what Disneyland is like?"

Oh god, maybe I'm pushing this too far. But it's like once a tiny truth tumbled out, I can't stop.

"Yeah. Is it really the happiest place on Earth?"

"I'm probably not the right person to ask."

"Why?"

He grins. "Because when I was twelve, I got mad at my mom for not taking me, so I went on my own."

"How'd you get there?"

"We had a driver."

"And?"

"And I liked it. But only for a little bit. When I started looking around, I realized how many families were there and how happy they looked together. I watched the moms take pictures of their kids and the dads go on the roller coasters and I just felt so overwhelmingly lonely."

"Oh. My dad's not around either," I offer. "He took off years ago."

He stares into my eyes. "Mine was never around *to* take off. My mom met him in Paris, at some business summit. They spent a week together. When he found out I was on the way . . . well, I suppose he wished my mom good luck and that was it. When I was a kid, sometimes I'd have this fantasy of just . . . *showing up* at his office."

"But you've never done it?"

He shrugs. "Why would I? It's not like I'm hard to find. If he wanted anything to do with me, I'd know it."

"So that's why your last name is the same as your grand-father's," I muse. "Because your mom never married?"

He nods. "And that's why I feel like I'm failing him. He's the closest thing to a father figure I've ever had. I want him to be proud of me."

"He will be," I say. "You'll figure it out."

"I just wish I'd never done all that stupid stuff in California. It seemed to change the way he viewed me."

"That's all behind you, though," I say. "He'll see that."

"What about you? Any wild phases?"

I smirk. "Not really. I did run away once."

"Oh?"

"I was already into history, you know? And then we were reading *From the Mixed-up Files of Mrs. Basil E. Frankweiler* at school, and I guess I got a little bit, uh, inspired."

"Never read it," he says, reaching down to scoop up a rock.

"Seriously? You're missing out."

He skips the stone across the water, and we both watch until it plinks under the surface. "What does it have to do with running away?"

"It's about a girl and her brother who decide to run away and live in a museum."

"Oh," he says, laughing. "Now I get it."

"Yeah. I thought it was the best idea I'd ever heard, so I packed a bag and hopped a city bus."

"How'd that work out?"

"It didn't." I grin. "It was six thirty on a Sunday evening, and the museum was closed. And I missed the last bus home. I had to call my mom. She was more relieved than angry, but I still got grounded for two weeks."

"So I guess neither of us should run away anytime soon, eh?"

I shake my head. "Nah, but I still want to see Disneyland."

"We'll go," he says with absolute sincerity. "Maybe during one of your semester breaks from college."

It's not supposed to be like this. It's not supposed to be quiet and sincere, and we're not supposed to be thinking of the future beyond the end of summer.

He turns and pulls me against him, talking into my hair. "You really are good for me," he whispers, his voice barely louder than the sea.

I lean into him, enjoying the warmth of his skin on mine. Moments later, we turn and stroll just far enough up the wet sand that we aren't in the water anymore.

We walk hand in hand, picking our way around everyone else. I know I shouldn't be here with him, where so many people can see us and take our pictures and sell them to some shoddy gossip rag, but I can't bring myself to go back to the car. To cut our time short.

"What happened with your best friend?" I finally ask. "I mean . . . how did it all go down?"

"Huh?"

"You said you realized he wasn't friends with you for the right reasons."

"Oh. Yeah."

"And it was after Nepal?"

"Yes."

"Sounds like it was a tornado," I say, looping my arm around his. "Changing everything so abruptly, I mean."

"That's what it felt like. He was with me the night I wrecked my car. Remember how I said it didn't faze me? It didn't faze him, either. And even though eventually I got it, he hasn't. He's still doing the same old thing."

I don't say anything. I just listen as the words spill out.

"The thing is, I wrecked the car and had to go to the hospital for a few hours for X-rays. He called me just as I was checking out to ask when I'd show up."

"He went to the party?"

"Yeah. He had a scrape on his forehead but no serious injuries, and when they carted me off, he just . . . called another friend and continued to the party."

"Wow."

"Yeah. And the thing is, who I was then . . . it didn't even bother me that much, that he went to the party while I went to the hospital. It wasn't until I got back and my quote-unquote friends threw me a 'Welcome Home' party that I completely dropped them."

"Why?"

"I tried to tell them about Nepal. I tried to talk about how we could make something big happen, how we were the perfect people to find ways to help them, and none of them wanted to listen. They wanted me to take another shot, another drink, to turn the music up."

"Hmm," I say, to indicate I'm listening.

"I realized our friendship had nothing to do with *me*, as a person. I was just someone to party with, someone to drive him around from one event to the next."

"Maybe it's a blessing, that you realized it all at once. In my case, my best friend is just . . . slowly drifting away," I say. "Sometimes, I think I've been replaced."

"Yeah?"

"Yeah. We've always been friends with Rena, but I never felt . . . *threatened* by her."

"And now you do?"

"Yeah. It's like almost every time I want to hang out with her, Rena's there. And they have all these inside jokes and they're going to see movies together I was supposed to see with her, and it just sucks."

"Hey, if anyone understands it, it's me."

"It's funny, isn't it?" I ask, turning to him. "How much we have in common."

He pulls my hands to him, cupping them together and holding them against his chest.

"You and I . . . we're the same," he says.

And as stupid as it is, he's right. We *are* the same.

I just have to figure out a way to tell him my real name so he still believes it.

Malik is the only guy in the world for me.

I can't lose him.

CHAPTER TWENTY-FIVE

Two days later, I've got my phone pressed to my ear, and I'm chewing on my bottom lip to keep from panicking.

I shouldn't be surprised.

I know I shouldn't be surprised, but I am.

"Send him away," I say, glancing out the curtains of my room even though they don't face the parking lot. All I can see is a big laurel bush.

My mom sighs. "I didn't know you put his name on the persona non grata list. I let him in because I knew he was the boy you went to prom with. I have to get to a meeting. Just come out and tell him why yourself, okay? I can't deal with this right now."

"I thought we had security for—"

But the line goes dead.

Ugh, how can my mom not realize that Hunter is the current bane of my existence?

I toss my phone onto my bed, leaving our apartment behind and taking the short walk to the front desk. It would be cool if I just "got lost" somewhere along the way, right? And not weird at all?

Ugh.

When I round the corner and Hunter spots me, he positively leaps to his feet. "Holly!"

I scowl. "Hunter, we've been through this. Call me Mathews, just like always. It *really* annoys me when you call me Holly."

"Sorry. *Mathews*."

"What are you doing here?"

He shrugs. "Was in the neighborhood, so thought I'd drop by and see what you were up to."

"No, you didn't. You thought you'd drop by and try to run into Malik."

He narrows his eyes. "Hey. We're friends too. I like you." He steps forward, reaching out to my cheek as if to . . . I don't know . . . caress my face?

I jerk back.

"Seriously, Hunter, you have to understand, you aren't wel—"

The front door dings, and I want to slump to the ground in despair as Malik walks into the building.

His eyes light up when he sees me. Then they slip over to Hunter, and it's like I can see him physically resisting the urge to roll his eyes. Hunter turns away from me, toward Malik, so I mouth *I know* to Malik over his shoulder and then *Sorry*.

Hunter does this weird rush-at-Malik-man-hug thing that is positively awkward, and Malik barely manages to disentangle himself.

"Hey, bro," Hunter says, sticking his fist out for a bump.

Seriously, does he think that if he physically touches Malik enough, it will result in fame by osmosis?

"Uh, hello," Malik says. Like being formal will make it clear they are not, in fact, bros. "What was your name again?"

I want to grin from ear to ear, but Hunter is all too quick to rush in and supply his name. Can't he take a hint?

Wow, I must have been blinded by his white teeth back when we dated or something, because I completely missed the fact that he is . . . intolerable.

I shove my hands into my pockets, only then realizing I'm wearing torn-up jeans and a purple T-shirt with a small bleach stain on one shoulder.

Oh, god. I did not plan to see Malik while dressed like this. I look like a homeless person.

"So what are you two up to today?" Hunter asks. "I thought we could—"

"Look, guy," Malik says. "I'm not sure how you knew to find us here, but—"

"Well, Mathews—"

"But," Malik says, more forcefully, "frankly, it is an invasion of privacy. I suggest you back off. I don't know you, you don't know me, and it should probably stay that way, okay?"

Hunter looks stricken, and I would almost feel sorry for him if, you know, he wasn't such a transparent jerk.

"Okay, okay, I'm sorry," he says. "I'll leave you two alone. But could I maybe just get one picture before you go?"

"Hunt—"

"It's okay," Malik says, resigned. I hate that jaded tone in his voice. It doesn't belong there. "That's fine. But then you go."

Hunter tosses me his phone so quickly, I nearly miss it and have to jump to keep it from crashing to the floor.

I switch on the camera, snap a quick pick of them—Hunter with his arm around Malik, of course—and then we're done.

"Okay, then, guys. See you later." Hunter retreats, slowly, like a puppy with his tail between his legs.

Malik and I turn away, exchanging a good-grief kind of look, and from the corner of my eye, I catch Hunter lingering in the space between the two sets of automatic doors.

I turn and glare, and he finally gets it, spinning on his heel and walking away.

Finally, Malik turns to me. "So, fourth floor? Want to join us for lunch again? Maybe Henrietta—"

"Actually, I was just leaving when I ran into him," I lie.

"Oh. All right."

"I'm just going to hang around for a minute in the lobby to give time for your new BFF to clear out."

He snorts, then pokes me in the ribs. "Seriously, I can't believe you dated that guy."

"Me either."

"Okay then, catch up later?"

"Mm-hmm," I say as he gives me a quick kiss, then slips away, heading down the hall.

I wait until he's disappeared into the elevator before I rush down the hall in the opposite direction, back to my room.

• • •

"I can't believe he sold me out. I mean, I should believe it. I really should. But I never thought he'd stoop to this level."

Alex throws herself down on her bed beside me, so we're stretched out on our stomachs, propped up on our elbows as we take in her laptop screen.

I'm staring at some TMZ rip-off, and there under the headline "Is Malik Buchannan Slumming It?" are Malik and I. I'm dressed in the ratty clothes I was wearing yesterday because, *hello*, I hadn't expected to see him. His clothes are well cut, expensive-looking even on the cell-phone-quality picture, and my torn-up jeans and purple T-shirt with the stain on one shoulder are painfully ugly in comparison.

God, I can't believe he saw me like that. How has he not yet noticed I'm a nobody? That I've never come from money, not even the kind Alex's family has?

Plus, ugh, his hair is so perfect, and I've got a greasy-looking ponytail.

"You didn't notice Hunter taking this picture?"

"I was kind of staring at Malik?" I say, motioning to the picture. "It's hard to pay attention to anything but him when he's in the room. I realized Hunter was kind of lingering, but it didn't occur to me he was snapping a picture of us. I thought he cared more about a picture of *himself* with Malik. I really didn't think he'd stoop to this level."

I go to roll off her bed and stand but miscalculate and just roll right off, falling to the ground with a heavy thump that nearly knocks the wind out of me.

Alex bursts into a cackling laugh, and I can't help but grin, even though I don't want to. "I can't believe you can laugh at a time like this," I say, trying to scowl. "As my best friend, you're supposed to sympathize with me here."

"Okay, okay," Alex says. "There are some silver linings, though."

"Please, point them out to me."

"Well, I mean . . ." Her voice trails off, and she clicks on the laptop. "*Celeb Scoops* doesn't know who you are. They just got ahold of the picture somehow."

"But how'd they get the picture without figuring out who I am?" I say, sitting up. "Surely, there's someone who would *pay* for the complete scoop."

"Hunter probably put the picture on Facebook or something and someone forwarded it along. Maybe someone who doesn't know who you are at all. He probably doesn't realize it's a big deal to put up pictures of Malik."

I sit up so that I can see her expression. "What he's done has fed the flames. Malik came up here to get away from the spotlight, and now Hunter's bringing it straight back to him."

Alex rolls onto her back, staring upward at the glittery stars, but she doesn't say anything. "What are you going to do?"

I sit cross-legged, rubbing my eyes. "I think . . . time is running out. Someone is going to figure out my real name, and then Malik is going to find out I've been lying to him. I need to tell him."

I half expect her to protest, to tell me not to jeopardize my romance, but she doesn't.

"I think you're probably right."

"I don't know how I'll do it."

"Umm . . . via text?"

I snort. "Oh, *hi*, Malik. Just FYI, I thought you should know my real name is Holly! Oh, yeah. And I'm always at Sunrise House because I live there! Kay, thanks, bye!"

Alex giggles. "Okay, okay, so you tell him in person. Cook him dinner or something first and butter him up."

"Yeah, in *your* kitchen? While he studies your family portraits?"

"Oh. Right. Hmm . . . ugh, he took a picture with Malik, too?"

I glance up. "Huh?"

"His new Facebook image is him and Malik."

I sit up taller and take in the picture on the screen.

"You're Facebook friends with him?"

"No, but Rena is. Maybe his profile is set to friends of friends or something."

My heart twists. "Are you sure it's not public?"

She raises a brow. "Um, no? How would I—"

"Log out and see if it still shows."

I climb to my feet and crawl closer to the bed just as she clicks the logout button, and . . .

Nothing changes.

"His freaking profile is public!"

Alex narrows her eyes. "Why is that a big deal?"

"Because people are going to see those photos and message him and dangle something in front of him to get him to tell. I am so screwed."

"Okay. Then I suggest you text Malik and set up a date. And tell him. Before someone else does."

I fall back against the floor, wishing I could sink right into the carpet and not face what I need to do next.

CHAPTER TWENTY-SIX

The next morning, I'm just about to step into the hall at Sunrise House, Alex and Rena trailing behind me, when Malik strolls by. Just as he turns and his eyes catch mine, I instinctively slam the door shut.

"What the—" Alex exclaims.

"It's Malik," I explain.

"Did he see?"

Then the knock comes.

"Oh my god, what do I do?" I ask.

"I mean, I hate to point out the obvious, but weren't you going to tell him?"

"Not like this!" I hiss. "I was going to do it tonight in a quiet, private place."

"Okay, okay," Alex says, throwing up her hands as her eyes go wide. "Don't panic. Sheesh. Let's just pretend *my* grandma lives here."

"He knows that's not true," I whisper, "or you wouldn't have told him you were going to hang out and play Candy Crush in your car a few weeks ago."

He knocks again. "Uh, Lucy?"

"So it's my grandma, then," Rena says, waving her hand like it's no big deal. "But you better open that door because he's going to figure out something's up."

I close my eyes and rake in a calming breath, then plaster a smile on my face and turn back to the entry, twisting the knob.

"Malik," I say, greeting him with a wide smile. "I didn't know you were here today."

"I was just leaving. What're you doing down here on the first floor?" he asks, glancing over my shoulder and into the apartment.

I'm seriously glad we don't have a giant portrait of me and my mom over the fireplace. *That* would be hard to explain.

"Um, just visiting with Rena and her grandma. We're on our way out the door, though," I say, stepping toward him and forcing him out of my way.

"Oh? Do you guys have plans?"

"Swimming," I say, pointing to the ties on my bikini top, which are poking out of my tank top. "We're heading to Alex's house."

"You guys can come to mine instead, if you want," he says. "We could do the pool or the lake, whichever you prefer."

"Oh, you don't have to—"

"Yes," Alex and Rena say in unison. I grit my teeth, forcing a smile on my face.

"Um, sure. That sounds great."

• • •

I'm sitting on the dock at Malik's house in my swimsuit, watching Rena and Alex, wondering how it is that Rena slid so easily into my place in Alex's life. They're both on floating loungers, arms dangling into the water.

I think they're trying to give me space, or something, so I can talk to Malik in private, but I can't get up the courage to pull him aside. I feel like I'm standing at the airplane door and I'm supposed to jump, but I don't trust that my parachute will work.

And I am not prepared to crash to the ground and lose Malik.

I sigh, closing my eyes against the glare and tip my head back against the heat of the afternoon sun. The lake water remaining in my hair has all but dried, and the ice in my once-cold lemonade has melted.

August. I'm not sure where the summer went. Ever since I met Malik, it's passed in a blur of dates and laughter and kissing. And now I have less than a week until I leave for college.

"So, how long have they been together?" Malik asks, dropping down onto the deck beside me. "They look happy."

"Who?" I ask, opening my eyes and shielding them against the glare.

"Rena and Alex."

I laugh. "They're not together, they're friends. I've known them both since the fourth grade."

He slides his sunglasses onto the top of his head and stares directly into my eyes with an intense look, like he's trying to get through to me. Or read my mind. Or . . .

"Why are you looking at me like that?" I whisper, the words sounding more annoyed than I mean them to. My heart seems to slow, as if my blood has turned to syrup and it can't quite keep up. "I'm telling you, they're not *together*."

He lets out a slow breath, and the realization that he's holding back hits me hard. It's like he's not sure how to break bad news to me.

Like I'm wrong.

"They're holding hands under the water," he says, lowering his voice.

My breathing goes shallow as I turn back to where they're floating, each with an arm dangling into the cool waters of Lake Washington.

I can't see their hands. Just where the water laps at their upper arms. I can't seem to move. I just stare into the murky depths, willing them to float closer, to let me see if what Malik's saying is true.

It can't be true. It just can't be. I would know.

"Sorry, I didn't mean to—"

"You're wrong," I say. "I would know. Alex would've told me."

As I say it, I flash back through all my memories of the last year.

Alex and Rena attending prom, saying they were going stag. They danced together. But girls dance together all the time. It doesn't mean anything.

They also bought each other corsages.

Holy crap, *they bought each other corsages!* I thought it was for fun, a way to make them feel like they weren't left out of the rite of passage just because they went without a date.

But what if they didn't go without a date after all?

I think of the way Alex had been avoiding my call after the movie-theater date with Malik, when Rena was in the background.

And how they were together at the coffee shop.

They're always together.

I thought Rena was replacing me as Alex's best friend. But this whole time . . .

"She never said," I say, and it sounds like the verbal equivalent of a toddler stomping her feet.

"You want to take the kayak out?" Malik asks, suddenly standing. "Maybe you could use a little fresh air. Um, I mean . . . breathing room."

I let him pull me to my feet and numbly follow, replaying my last few hangouts with Rena and Alex. The way they stood close together at the coffee shop and how Rena fell against Alex when she was laughing really hard. The way Alex opened the car door for Rena when they pulled up at Alex's house the last time we were there.

The way they made those bracelets for each other instead of making their own.

Malik leads me to a boathouse next to the dock. A moment later, he's holding out a life vest so I can stick my arms through it. He clicks on the snaps. He's handling it all like he knows I'm moving on autopilot, that my brain isn't completely functioning.

And then I'm climbing behind him into the second seat of a double-seated kayak and we're pushing away from the dock.

I halfheartedly paddle as we leave his house behind, letting Malik do most of the work. Until he finally stops and we just float across the rippling water.

"Lucy?"

I close my eyes against the name, suddenly feeling over-whelmed. By the boy who thinks he knows me. By the friend I thought I knew.

Maybe everyone has a secret.

"Yeah?" I say a heartbeat later.

"What are you thinking right now?"

I laugh, a painful, half-amused, half-hurt laugh. "It's stupid."

"I doubt that."

"Well . . . a big part of me is relieved. That's what I'm think-ing. That I'm relieved."

"Why?"

"I've been worrying all summer that Alex was replacing me as her best friend, but it's something else entirely."

"Fair enough," he says, glancing back at me over his shoulder.

"Why wouldn't she tell me?"

"She's probably scared."

"Of?"

"Losing you. You're scared of that yourself, aren't you? Scared that she doesn't need you as a friend like you need her."

I'm glad he can't really see my expression, so I can sit alone with my flood of thoughts. I thought I knew her. I thought . . .

"I guess," I say. "I kind of figured since they were going to college together that I was just being left out of that. Of their plans together. I think I've just been blind."

"Maybe we should go back and you can talk to her."

"Or maybe not?" I say.

He chuckles. "Do you really want to put it off? We can stay out here for a while, you know. It's a big lake."

"Yes. No. Maybe."

I need to spend today talking to Malik, telling him the truth. But it's all I can do to process this other kind of truth.

Malik knows enough to not respond. He just gently paddles in a way that doesn't seem to take us closer to the dock *or* farther away. Just allows us to drift like this, under the searing summer sun. Occasionally, the waves of passing boats roll toward us, and we bounce along the surface like a fisherman's bob.

"Okay," I say, finally gathering my courage. "Yeah. Let's go back."

The dock comes up too fast. Then the kayak bumps against the lake bottom near the shore, and Malik climbs out, pulling it onto the sand with me in it.

He gives me a hand, and I clamber to my feet. He releases my hand with a quick, reassuring squeeze, picking up the kayak and heading to the boathouse. I'm stand there on the shore, staring out across the water at Alex and Rena.

They are still there, floating along on their loungers, tanning or sleeping or maybe really holding hands, like Malik says. I've never wished so much to be able to see through the water. Even though it all makes sense, I still can't quite believe it. I can't stop looking for something—some kind of real confirmation that what Malik has said is true.

The way the dock and the sun reflect across the surface, it's impossible to know if he's right.

But what he said . . . when I heard it . . .

It was like everything clicked together in a way it never has. And though I have to do this—have to ask her if it's true—the doubts slipped away somewhere between the dock and the open water.

"Alex?" I walk barefoot down the dock. She twists around on the lounger, looking at me almost upside down.

"Mm-hmm?" she responds sleepily.

"Can you come help me with something please?"

"Sure," she says, sitting up a little more and dropping her feet into the water. If she was holding Rena's hand, it doesn't show.

She kicks her way over to the dock, water splashing up and over Rena, who seems oblivious to anything but the sun and a nap.

"Don't float away," I call out to Rena as Alex climbs up the steel ladder. I take her lounger, tossing it down on the middle of the dock.

"What do you need?" Alex says, water dripping onto the deck boards.

"Um, it's up at the house. I thought we could . . . bring down snacks," I say.

"Awesome. I'm starving."

We follow an aggregate walkway up to a set of steps winding past a tennis court. We skirt the little waterfall feature, and it changes colors as I walk by, from a muted blue to a vibrant green.

Eventually, we slip inside, where the air is instantly cooler. I walk to the kitchen, Alex on my heels, and stop when I'm at the fridge. I grip the cool steel handle but don't open the door.

I linger, staring at the blurry outline of myself reflected in the steel surface.

"Uh, Holly?"

"Do you love her?" I ask, unable to turn around.

"What?" I can't see her face, but the slight shrieking tone to her voice tells me everything I need to know.

She's not confused. She's shocked.

"Rena. Do you love her?"

I remain staring at the fridge. Staring, Staring, Staring. Until a warm hand rests on my shoulder, turning me to face Alex.

There's no fear on her face, just . . . sympathy. For me?

It hits me all at once—the realization that she's worried she's betrayed me. Hurt me.

"How did you figure it out?" she asks softly.

"I didn't."

"But—"

"Malik thought I knew."

"Oh," she says as her face falls.

"I don't care," I rush to say.

She blinks. "You don't?"

"No. I mean . . . I care, but not about that. I care because I thought I was losing you as my best friend. I care because I thought you were replacing me." I lean back against the fridge, resting my head. "I care because you thought you couldn't trust me enough to tell me the truth."

"Of course I trust you," Alex says. She turns to the countertop behind her, hopping up and letting her legs dangle down.

The surreality of the moment—of sitting in this kitchen in a mansion talking to Alex about this—washes over me. All the times we talked about me not being myself around Malik, and Alex held this secret of her own.

"But you didn't tell me."

"I haven't told anyone."

"Not even your mom?" Alex is close with her mom. She spends so much time with her. More than I've ever spent with my own mom.

She shakes her head. "I don't even know what it is, this thing between me and Rena. But yes, I love her. We figured we could go away to college and figure it out there. And if it becomes a real thing . . . a lasting thing . . . then we'll tell people."

"So she's *not* my replacement."

"She's something else," Alex says, smiling. "I would never replace you, Holly. You will *always* be my best friend."

"Promise?" I say, suddenly feeling ridiculously, stupidly happy.

"Promise," she says, extending her pinkie finger.

I step forward, and we pinkie-swear like we used to in the sixth grade. And for the first time in a long time, I'm not worried about losing my best friend.

"Hey," a voice calls out, and I twist around to see Malik slipping inside the doors. "Everything cool?"

He eyeballs me, as if to make sure I'm okay. In this moment, I realize how much he cares about me. As a person.

And how much I love him.

I grin. "Yeah. Never better."

As he crosses the kitchen, Alex steps away, sauntering back to the patio. "I'm going to go back down to the lake. You guys coming down?"

"Yeah, in a bit," he answers, not quite taking his eyes off me.

He walks to the kitchen, and I take a tiny step back as he gets closer, placing one of his hands on each side of my hips and pinning me between him and the kitchen cabinet, a flirty smile on his lips. "I have an idea."

"Oh?"

"Yeah. We're going out tonight."

"Where?"

"Someplace quiet."

Someplace quiet? It'll be the perfect place to tell Malik the truth.

"Okay. Does it have a dress code?"

"No, but you should still dress up," he says, grinning.

"I can handle that. What time?"

"Six. Gives Alex and Rena time to swim as long as they want, and then you guys can head out and you can get ready."

"Deal."

CHAPTER TWENTY-SEVEN

I'm lying on my bed, my phone still gripped in my hand, when his reply finally comes in.

I sit up and unlock the screen.

710 Broadway, Tacoma

I blink. Tacoma is farther than I expected, a good forty-five minutes south of Seattle. I type back, What's at 710 Broadway?

The response comes just moments later: You'll see. Meet me there at eight thirty.

Eight thirty. That gives me an hour to get ready and an hour to get to the address.

I flick open a new text and send it to Alex.

Thanks again for letting me borrow your car. I'm heading out in an hour to meet Malik.

My phone chirps moments later.

Oyy . . . You're still telling him the truth, right?

Just seeing her words on the screen makes my stomach twist.

Yep.

I go to my closet and start digging through my clothes, searching for one of the outfits Alex gave me. I land on a silk blouse and a little black skirt.

Hopefully, this little surprise date isn't, like, rock climbing or basketball or something. He did say to dress nice, though.

It takes me thirty minutes to curl my hair and twist it up over my head, slip into the new outfit, and find a pair of heels that look like they *maybe* weren't purchased at Target.

I give myself a once-over in the mirror. I'm tempted to take it all off and switch to clothes that look more like me. Tonight's about coming clean, after all.

But I can't quite bring myself to slip out of the outfit. I feel good in it. Confident.

Just like Alex knew I would, when she thrust all those bags at me.

At a quarter to eight, I'm in Alex's car flying down the road, drumming my fingers on the steering wheel as anticipation builds in my chest.

Broadway is one of the main drags in Tacoma, an eclectic mix of luxury condos, hotels, museums, and old factory buildings.

And as I slow, coming up on the 700 block of Broadway, I realize my destination is an old building, faded paint on the exterior proclaiming BEASLEY'S FURNITURE COMPANY.

Huh? What the heck are we doing at an abandoned warehouse?

I pull to a stop in the darkened shadow of the building, peering up at it. Unlike the converted lofts downtown, this one is an empty shell, with busted windows like rows of broken teeth. I'm staring up at it, wondering if Malik somehow typed the wrong address, when someone taps on my window.

I nearly jump out of my seat, but relief whooshes through me when I see his face. "I think I just had a heart attack," I say as I push open the door.

"Sorry," he says, giving me a sheepish grin.

"This place is kind of creepy-looking."

"It's not so bad. Come on."

"Where are we going?"

"It's a surprise."

He interlaces his fingers with mine, tugging me toward the brick shell of a building. I decide not to question him and simply follow along, wondering what in the world could be inside this place. It's an odd location for a date, but then, his choice in dates has never been conventional. For all I know he hired a band and a caterer.

It's not as dark as I thought it would be once we step inside. Old wooden floors creak as we cross the expanse, stepping through slanted splashes of fading sunlight. He pulls me toward a doorway that has been propped open.

The stairwell is a little darker, but at each landing, another door is propped open, leaving us with enough light to navigate the steps. But the final door, at the top, is closed.

He turns me to face him, pulling something out of his back pocket. "Okay, you have to trust me here," he says. Before I can protest, he slips a silk blindfold over my face, gently tying it behind my head. The fabric is cool against my skin and blocks out every last ray of light, plunging me into darkness.

I take in deep breath, relieved when he takes my hand again.

I allow him to pull me forward, and he must be opening the door because the hinges squeal, echoing down the stairwell. "Watch your step; there's a little lip on the threshold."

I sort of shuffle forward, gripping his hand tighter, and then the cool night air kisses my cheeks and exposed arms and I know we're outside. Wait, outside? Shouldn't we be *inside* when we exit the stairs?

"Okay, stop right there." He drops my hand, then grips my upper arms and turns me.

He steps forward, so close I can smell the faint trace of his cologne, and his arms brush over my shoulders as he reaches behind me to remove the blindfold.

It slides off my eyes with a whisper of silk.

And my jaw drops.

We're on a rooftop overlooking the Thea Foss waterway, where sailboats glide from their docks out into the Puget Sound. Christmas lights are strung from the edges of the roof to an antenna pole attached above the stairwell, creating a sort of circus-tent roof effect.

And in the center of it all sits a table for two, draped in a white tablecloth and topped with a flickering candle

"Now I know you question my elaborate dates, but I hope this one still counts as real. Because I didn't hire anyone or spend a ton of money." He grins. "Well, I did spend fifty dollars on a waffle iron."

Malik doesn't take his eyes off my face as I take in his words. Take in the beauty of the rooftop. The romance of it.

It's like something from a movie.

"Happy National Waffle Day," he says, waving his arms with a flourish.

I laugh. "National Waffle Day?"

He grins, leaning forward to kiss me. "You like holidays. And there aren't that many to choose from in August."

He leads me past the table in the center of the Christmas-light-tent, to a much more utilitarian table I hadn't noticed until now.

Filling the surface is a waffle iron, waffle mix, eggs, milk, a carafe of orange juice, and a clearly handmade cake, with swirls of buttercream frosting and crooked lettering.

Lettering which proudly states, HAPPY NATIONAL WAFFLE DAY.

I'm so stunned and speechless that I can't seem to get any words to form. I can't believe he went to these lengths for me. Can't believe he finally stopped opening up his wallet and got creative instead.

Because of my lie.

Guilt burns in my stomach, but I muster what I hope is a grateful, dazzling smile. "You are amazing," I say. "Really, truly amazing."

"I hope you're hungry," he says, reaching for the mix.

"Starving."

The cool breeze coming off the water picks up, and I shiver.

"There's a blanket on those chairs," he says, jutting a thumb over his shoulder as he sets about mixing the batter.

"You really thought of everything," I say. "How did you even find this place?"

"My mother's company owns it. They're going to turn this whole place into luxury lofts."

"Ah," I say, wrapping a warm red blanket around my shoulders. "So her company does buildings up here, too? Not just California?"

He nods. "Yeah. It started out as just a small offshoot of my grandpa's company, but she's grown it. She has projects up and down the West Coast. She's done pretty well with buildings like this."

He sounds proud of her. In the same way I'm proud of my mom for getting her job at Sunrise House. I don't know whether this means we're completely different or entirely the same.

He pours batter into the waffle iron and turns back to me. As he peers into my eyes, I want to blurt it all out. I want to tell him I'm Holly, not Lucy; that I don't live at Alex's house; and that it's not my car parked down there at the curb.

"Here's to celebrating many more holidays together."

As he steps closer, taking my chin in his hand and tilting my head back, I close my eyes and kiss him back with everything I have.

Unbearable sadness wells in my throat, and when he pulls away, he begins to smile, but then his face freezes.

"What?"

I swallow, willing my vision to stop glittering with tears. "I have to tell you something."

"Okay . . . ," he says, his voice trailing off. He takes a tiny step back, and I don't know if it's involuntary on his part or what, but that tiny move sends my nerves into panic mode.

The silence settles in until I can't handle it anymore. I blurt it out. "My name's not Lucy."

He freezes, his eyes narrowed and lips pressed into a thin line, as if the words don't seem to make sense.

"But—" he says, and then stops, as if he doesn't know what to say.

"It's Holiday," I say, forcing the words to spill. "And yeah, I like holidays, but in a normal way." I rake in a breath, trying to calm my hammering heart, but it does nothing. "They all call me Holiday because it's my *name*. I'm Holiday Mathews, and I *live* at Sunrise House."

"*What?*" He furrows his brow, and that gleam of mistrust sparks in his eyes. "How is that possible? It's a retirement home."

I blink as the tears brim, one trailing down my cheek. I hate the look on his face. I hate that he takes a step back as my betrayal registers. "My mom's the leasing manager. The one who convinced your mom that your grandpa should move in. Until she got the job, we lived in a series of crappy apartment complexes."

"No. That can't be. Henrietta—"

I shake my head, my lip trembling. "Is not my grandmother. We're not even related. She's called me Lucy since the day I met her. I remind her of her granddaughter."

He takes another step back, bigger this time, as if I've slapped him. His face grows ashen. He begins to shake his head, slowly at first, but then with increased speed over and over and over. Like he wants to deny my confession. Like he refuses to believe it.

"I'm sorry," I whisper through my tears. "I wanted to tell you, but I thought you'd stop talking to me."

"Because you thought I was that shallow?" he asks bitingly. "That I only gave you the time of day because I thought you were rich enough? Do you really think that little of me?"

"No," I say. "*No*. It wasn't like that."

In this moment, I know. I waited too long. I lied too much.

I've lost him.

I bite my lip, hard, to stop it from trembling. "I didn't even know who you were when all this started. When Henrietta walked in and called me Lucy."

"You've had a lot of time to get to know me," he snaps back. "The time to *tell* me."

"I know."

He blinks, and I can see him turning over everything in his mind, every day we spent together, every element of my identity. "So that house we went to? The Craftsman?"

"Was Alex's."

"So that was *her* mom. And *her* bedroom."

I nod.

"Was anything real?"

I try to swallow the lump in my throat. "I never lied about what I think about you. About how I feel about you."

"Just about who you are!" he says, throwing his hands up in the air. "I told you *everything*. Things I've never told anyone."

"I'm sorry," I say again, my heart breaking. Because everything he's saying is true. With each secret he shared, I lied. Again and again and again. "I wanted to tell you the truth, but I was afraid you'd—"

"What? Judge you? Did you really think I'm the kind of guy who can only be with someone of my—" He stops.

"Class? Wealth? No. Not anymore. But I do think you'd only be with someone you can trust. By the time I figured that out, it was too late. I knew I'd betrayed you."

The breeze kicks up again, and the circus-dome lights flutter in the breeze, bouncing in a way that would feel magical if it weren't so tragic.

"Please," I say, my desperation evident in the words, "you have to understand I never meant to hurt you. I've just been so afraid to tell you because *I love you*. I've never *loved* a guy before and it scares me. And I know other people—"

"People always lie," he says, his voice cracking with emotion. "Always. I should've known you wouldn't be the exception."

And then he spins on his heel and leaves me there on the rooftop, where I stop fighting and just let my tears fall, one after another.

CHAPTER TWENTY-EIGHT

I slip into our darkened apartment, creeping quietly through the door. I turn back to hit the deadbolt, twisting it slowly, so as not to make a big clank.

"Coming in late, aren't you?"

I leap into the air, whirling around as my heart thunders to life. "Geez, Mom! You scared the heck out of me!"

She's sitting in the big leather recliner, cross-legged, an iPad on her lap. I blink. She looks comfortable with the luxury. It's the way she should always look—in purple pajamas she bought only a month ago, a glass of wine beside her, her hair tumbling down around her shoulders, and the lamp set on low.

Success looks good on her.

"You scared me," I say, dropping my purse onto the counter.

"I could say the same."

"Uh, how did I scare you?"

"I figured you were in your room this whole time. I only just got in a half hour ago."

I walk to the cupboard, grabbing a glass and filling it with water. "Nope."

"Where've you been?" she asks, sliding the iPad off her lap.

"Out."

"With?"

I don't answer right away.

I'm tired of lying. And the gig is up anyway.

"Malik," I say, turning back to my mother.

Her eyes narrow, as if she's trying to place the name. And when she does, she sits back. "So that's still a thing, huh?"

I blink away the tears that want to well all over again. I'm not doing this in front of my mom. "Well, it was. Until an hour ago."

She leans forward, setting her elbows on her knees and steepling her hands.

"I see. What happened?"

I play with the bracelet on my wrist, the one I made at Alex's house, afraid to meet my mom's eyes.

"Holl?"

I finally glance up at her. "Remember how I said Charles Buchannan didn't know I was related to you?"

"Yes," she says, slowly, like she knows the real reveal is still coming.

"Well, I didn't tell Malik either."

"Okay."

"As in . . ." I blow out a breath, my cheeks puffing out. "As in, until an hour ago, he didn't know I lived here. Or that I don't come from money." Finally, I glance up and meet her eyes. "Or that my name is not Lucy."

Her lips part a fraction of an inch.

"Yeah. I was with Henrietta when we met."

"I take it the truth didn't go over so well?"

"No. People . . . they lie to him. Use him. And now, he thinks I'm one of them." I walk to the couch, sitting down and putting my feet up.

"I see," my mom says.

"And now I'm in love with him, and—" I stop when I see the look on her face. "What?"

"Nothing."

"Tell me."

"It's just that you're not a little girl anymore. I mean, it sounds like you screwed up, but you're out there, making your own decisions. This time next week, you're not even going to be under my roof. And on top of that, you've fallen in love with *Malik Buchannan*."

She says his name like I would've, three months ago. Like I'm more impressed by his reputation and not *him*.

"I know, it's stupid."

"It's funny. I figured *he* would break *your* heart, and here we are, discussing how you screwed up. I never saw *this* coming."

I lie down on the couch next to her recliner and rest my feet on the armrest. Without a word, my mom leans over and runs her fingers against the bare soles of my feet.

When I was little, before my dad bailed and things got tough, I used to do this every night. We'd watch some silly shows, and she'd let me prop my feet on her lap. She's rub my feet and I'd complain about math homework or mean girls or crappy PE class.

"How am I going to tell him the truth?" I ask. "I hate that our relationship started with such a stupid lie. I hate that I thought I needed to be rich like him to impress him."

"And you don't think that's the case now?"

"No. It couldn't be further from the truth. If anything, he wishes he could shed his lifestyle and be a nobody."

"So the problem is?"

"The lie itself. Not *what* I lied about. Just that I lied."

"Oh."

I blow out a breath, sinking farther into the couch. "Yeah."

"I don't think I'm any help there," she offers. "But we could make cookies."

I purse my lips, relishing the feeling of her short fingernails scraping the sole of my foot. "I mean . . . they *almost* solve everything, so . . ."

She chuckles, sliding my feet off her lap. "Come on. I bought some butterscotch chips a few days ago."

"Magic words," I say, following her across the living room. Somehow, I feel like the cookies will help. We used to spend our evenings baking silly things from scratch. It was the only time she would let me stay up late.

"So what is it you like about this boy?" she asks, grabbing the butterscotch chips out of a cupboard.

I walk to the fridge, pulling out the eggs and butter. "He just . . ." My voice trails off. "See, he tried really hard to impress me on our first couple of dates."

"Boys always do that." She grins. "I think it makes them feel better, if we're impressed."

"I know, but the thing is, I never wanted that. It made me uncomfortable, actually."

"Okay . . . ," she says, setting two bowls on the countertop.

"So anyway, I realized he just assumed that's what a girl wants, you know? Extravagant stuff like your dating shows."

My mom gets this dreamy look, staring off into the distance. "I'd love just *one* of those dates."

"Right. But not if it's the sort he took every other girl on."

"Oh," she says, snapping out of her daydream, realizing she's stopped stirring the dough. "Yeah, sure."

"That's how I realized I loved him."

"The fact that you hated the dates he took you on?" She puts a half stick of butter in the microwave, setting it for twenty seconds.

"No. The fact that I realized what I really wanted was to sit on some park bench and talk. Or go for a drive. Or . . . anything. What I really wanted, at the end of the day, was him. It was never the money or shutting down an entire movie theater for a private viewing or—"

"He did that?"

"Yes. Redmond Town Center."

She whistles, long and low, pulling the butter from the beeping microwave.

"Yeah. The thing is, I loved it best when he just told me about himself. Genuine stuff."

"He sounds like a nice guy," my mom says, whipping the butter into the brown sugar.

"That's the point," I say, rubbing my eyes. "He *is* a nice guy. I'm the one who is not so nice."

"He'll see that you are," my mom says, turning the whisk in circles. "How can he not?"

I smile, pouring flour into a bowl. "I guess I *am* pretty awesome," I say.

"Which reminds me," my mom says, rinsing her fingers off and drying them on a nearby towel. "I have a gift for you."

"Oooh, a gift!" I say, dusting my fingers off, excited to think about something—anything—other than Malik.

"I'll be right back."

She leaves the kitchen and disappears into her bedroom. I feel a little awkward standing there, leaning against the countertop . . . waiting.

But then she emerges, a small box in hand.

"Here."

I round the kitchen counter, following her over to the dining room table. The wrapping paper is blue and silver, the same as my high school colors. I slide my fingers over the ribbon. It feels like silk.

"Thank you," I say.

"You can thank me after you open it, if you like it."

"I know. But I mean thank you for *everything*. You've always been there."

"You're welcome," she says, beaming. "Don't think I don't know that you've made sacrifices too. You believed in me, just like I believe in you."

I slip the ribbon off the package, glancing back at my mother before ripping off the wrapping paper.

Inside is a small pendant. A silver sun.

"Oh my gosh," I say, holding it up. "Mom, this is amazing."

"I thought it would remind you of me. Since, hopefully, I'll pass probation in a few weeks and then I'll always be at Sunrise House. Maybe it'll keep you in line," she says, grinning.

I laugh. "It's beautiful. I love it."

"You deserve it. You've waited all this time for my ship to come in, and it arrives in a few weeks. So now it's your turn."

I rush to my mother, throwing my arms around her. "I'm so proud of you," I say, my voice muffled against her hair.

"I'm supposed to be saying that to you."

"I know, but I don't care."

"What did I do to deserve a daughter like you?"

I pull away, beaming at her. "You gave up everything to give me a good life. And now it's your turn."

We hug again. When we finally pull apart, I pick up the tiny velvet box. "I'm tired, so I'm going to go to bed. Maybe you could save me a few of those cookies?"

"Sure. And good luck smoothing things over with Malik."

I walk away, her words ringing in my ears.

I'm going to need every bit of luck I can find. I doubt he's going to talk to me.

Ever again.

CHAPTER TWENTY-NINE

A few days later, Alex is sitting on my suitcase as I struggle to
zip it, taking out all my frustration and anxiety on one tiny little
scrap of metal.

"Whoa there, Hulk," she says, batting my hand away.
"There's a sock stuck in the zipper."

I sit back and blow out a breath, trying to calm my frazzled
nerves. She quickly tucks the sock farther into my bag, then zips
it up. "Ta-da!"

"I don't know why you're so calm," I say, trying to ignore
the bare walls and the empty drawers around me. Trying to pretend today is *not* the day I climb into my car and drive away and
don't come back for almost three full months, when Thanks-
giving rolls around.

"I'm only going to school an hour from here. You're the one
moving three hundred miles away." She gets off my suitcase,

standing up to survey my empty room. "And *I* didn't just break up with my boyfriend."

"That's because it would be impossible when you, in fact, have a girlfriend," I say, flopping down on my bare mattress.

Alex swats my leg. "Don't be all grumpy now."

"Sorry. I just hate the idea of leaving this place with things just kind of hanging out there."

"That's because you've been holding out hope this whole week that you'd see him and win him back, and now you're going to have half the state between you."

"I know. But he's not returning my calls or my texts. I just wish he'd let me explain, you know? I didn't mean for it all to go down like this. Once I leave, it's over. Done. Finito."

"Give him time to cool off. A few weeks or something. And if you're still not over it, call him."

"I don't think it will matter. He turned his back on his best friend, too. He doesn't trust people, and I proved why."

"He's bound to miss you, Holls. Just leave him a voice mail or something. Explain yourself. At the very least, it'll get it off your chest."

I frown. "You're good at this. You should be a psychologist."

"Maybe if Dr. Phil retires, I'll take his job." She slides her phone out of her pocket. "Ugh, I've gotta get going. My mom's taking me shopping for dorm room decorations. You wanna go?"

I shake my head. "Nah, I have a few more things I want to get done today. We can meet up in the morning before I head out."

"Okay. See ya later," she says, leaving my room.

It's weird, but once she's gone, the emptiness of my room starts to get under my skin. It's not like I packed up every last thing I own or anything. But we haven't lived here that long and I don't have that much stuff, so it seems too empty, like I didn't spend the last five-plus months here, like it's not really my home at all.

I roll over onto my stomach, sliding my laptop off the night-stand and popping it open.

I open a blank e-mail, filling in Malik's e-mail address. The one I've never used.

Yet.

I couldn't e-mail him when he first gave me his address because my name would show up, so I just saved it in my address book.

I click a couple of times, and then I'm staring at a blinking cursor. My fingers hover over the keyboard, uncertainty swirling through me. But I have to try.

Malik,

I'm sorry. I know I said it already, but I need you to know that I mean it. I never wanted to hurt you. You're the last person in the world I'd hurt, because you're the first person I've ever fallen in love with.

I've spent my life feeling not good enough, feeling like I was less than everyone else, and I guess when you looked at me that first day, something sparked to life, and I was too scared of losing it to think logically. I enjoyed every minute I spent with you, and I wish I could go back and fix all this. I wish you'd forgive me. But I get it. I understand that it's an impossible wish.

I want you to know, though, that I believe in you. You're going to do big things with your life.

Forever yours,
Holly

PS: No matter how mad you are, click on the link below. I saw it yesterday and I thought of you immediately. Maybe it'll give you an idea or two.

Before I can get too nervous and back out, I click Send and slap the laptop shut. The sound seems to echo, ripping across the empty room like cannon fire. Like I've just officially said good-bye to the only boy I've ever loved.

It's physically painful.

I sigh, rolling off my bed and to my feet. I grab my last suitcase, wheeling it over and setting it next to the door of our apartment.

Only one thing left to do.

I leave our unit, heading to the elevator and hitting the Up button. When it arrives, I step inside and press the button for the fourth floor, dread filling me.

I have to say good-bye to Henrietta. Or, at least, good-bye for now. Otherwise she'll call the front desk and want me to walk her dog or hang out, and I can't handle the idea of someone else telling her I'm leaving.

I've been completely putting it off, but now's the time. I don't know how she'll react. If saying good-bye to *Lucy* will hurt. Or if maybe she'll just forget about it tomorrow and wonder where the heck I am again.

No matter what, it just seems wrong to leave without a word.

At Henrietta's door, I knock softly, then push it open a crack, leaning closer. "Henrietta?"

"Come on in," she calls out.

I find her sitting at one end of her oversized sofa, a coffee mug in hand, a soap opera blaring on the TV.

"Hey, sweetie," she says, beaming. She picks up the remote, pressing pause. The woman on screen freezes, her eyes comically large. "Coffee's hot if you want some."

"Uh, no, I'm okay." I don't think coffee pairs well with dread and guilt. "I wanted to talk to you, actually."

"About what?"

I sit down at the other end of the couch, turning to face her. "Um, well, I'm leaving in the morning. For college. So I'm not going to be around—"

"Oh!" she interrupts, setting her coffee down on the side table. "Of course. I have something for you."

She scoops her purse up off the floor at her feet, digging into the enormous handbag and producing a pale green envelope. The kind for greeting cards. "Here."

I accept the card. There's nothing scrawled on the outside, but it's sealed. I flip it over and rip it open, exposing the edges of red cardstock.

I slide it out and find the word CONGRATULATIONS! scrawled across the front in silver glitter. I glance up at Henrietta, taking in her eager expression, then back at the card as I swing it open.

I'm so proud of you, the card says, and Henrietta has signed it.

A slip of paper falls onto my lap, and I pick it up, the dread thickening to a heavy weight in my gut.

It's a check. She's giving me a check for graduation, and now I have to tell her I'm not Lucy, that I can't accept a check, or she'll get confused about balancing her checkbook or something, and wonder why her granddaughter never used the money.

I unfold the check, and two words jump out at me. Two tiny words that mean everything.

She's made the check out to Holiday Mathews.

She's made the *ten-thousand-dollar check* out to *Holiday FREAKING Mathews.*

Tears spring into my eyes and I glance up at her, taking in her toothy grin.

"You knew," I whisper, the truth hitting me hard, the lump growing in my throat.

She nods.

"But I thought you were confused. I thought—"

"It slipped out, the first time I called you Lucy. A simple mistake." Her smile is wide and apologetic.

It's hard to breathe. "But when I told you I wasn't her, that she had died, you cried. Like you were just finding out for the first time."

She shakes her head. "That wasn't it. It just . . . hits hard some days, you know? I lost my daughter when she was forty. Ten years before I moved here. And then after I moved in, my granddaughter would visit me all the time. She was all I had left. When she was killed in that wreck . . . it hit so hard. I didn't want to be alone in this world." She runs a shaky hand through her short, permed hair. "I hadn't spoken her name in two years, and then you walked into my apartment. You reminded me of her. I said her name before I caught myself. You corrected me, and it hit me all over again, that I was living here alone, that she never *would* walk in that door. I had no family left."

She purses her lips, staring downward, as if she feels guilty. "You really do look like her, especially when you smile. And then two weeks later, when I said it again on accident, you answered to her name. Pretended to be her. So I let you think I was confused, because . . ." She sighs. "I'm sorry, dear, but I was rather using you. I liked pretending you're my granddaughter, that I have someone left."

I grin then, through the tears. "Oh, Henrietta. We may not share blood, but it would be an honor to be your granddaughter." I hold the card out to her. "But you don't have to give me this. You don't owe me."

"And what would you have me do, leave all my money for the bank to squabble over when I'm gone? I want you to have this little bit. I want you to get your education and do something amazing with your life. You're a good person, Holiday, and you deserve it."

And that's it. My name on her lips makes me burst into tears, and I move over, hugging her for all I'm worth.

Twenty minutes later, and mostly dry-eyed, I'm walking to the elevator. Just as I pass Charles's door, it clicks open, and he steps into the hallway.

I hesitate, taking a stutter step, and meet his eyes.

He scowls, and I know immediately that Malik told him the truth about me. "You."

"Uh, yeah. Me."

I shove my hands into the back pockets of my jeans, staring back at him, waiting for him to call me out.

"Why?" he finally says.

"I wanted to be good enough," I say, sighing. "It wasn't some grandiose plan, though. It just sort of happened."

"I grew up poor, girl. You didn't need a name and fake money to impress my family."

I chew on my lip, my eyes downcast. "I know that now."

With that, he pushes past me, heading toward the elevator. I stand still, watching him go, until he presses the elevator button and glances back at me. "Well?"

"Well, what?" I ask.

"You coming down to lunch, or not?" the faintest of smiles twitching at his lips.

"Wait, you don't hate me?" I ask, walking closer.

He shrugs. "I've known some underhanded people in my day. You're not one of them."

"Oh." My heart soars. Charles forgives me? How is that possible?

The doors open with a *ding*, and we step inside. I try not to stare at him, but instead give up, turning to face him. "Does this mean Malik—"

"What he thinks of you is his own business," Charles says.

"Oh. Right," I say, and a little bit of the hope fizzles out.

"Give him time," Charles says. "He's even more stubborn than me."

"Hard to believe," I joke.

And he laughs. *Charles laughs.* I try to think of a time I've ever heard so much as a chuckle from him, but I come up blank. And when I meet his eyes, I can't help but grin back.

By the time the elevator doors open and I step out onto the ground floor, some tiny bit of my heart heals.

I don't know if Malik is ever going to forgive me. But if Charles can . . . maybe . . . *maybe* there's still hope.

CHAPTER THIRTY

A couple of weeks later later, I'm climbing one of the many hills on the Washington State University campus. Maybe I should've taken a PE credit this year, based on all my huffing and puffing, but I'm almost to my dorm room, so I can just pass out there instead.

My phone vibrates in my pocket, and I shift my backpack to the other arm, digging the phone out of my WSU hoodie.

"Yeah?" I say, clicking Accept.

"I'm *official*!" my mother yells into my ear so loudly, I wince and pull the phone back for a second.

"Wow, really?" I say, once my ear stops ringing. "So they signed off on your probationary period?"

"Yes! I'm a full-time, permanent employee now. If they want to fire me, they've gotta work for it."

I laugh. "Congrats, Mom. That's awesome."

"Thank you! I'm going out tonight to celebrate, and—" My phone beeps, interrupting her.

"Oh, hold on, I think Alex is calling me. We were going to catch up on how her classes are going."

"Okay, talk to you later, sweetie."

"Yeah, I'll call you back! Love you," I say, pulling the phone away from my ear.

It's not until after I tap Accept that the name on the screen registers.

Malik.

I stare at my phone in shock, gripping it so hard my fingers go pale, and my heart climbs up my throat.

"Aren't you going to answer?" a familiar voice calls out.

I whirl around, expecting him to be standing behind me on the pathway, but it's just another student in a WSU T-shirt, hustling past me with an armful of books.

I put the phone to my ear, wondering if he'll be able to hear my pounding pulse through the phone . . . or from wherever he's standing. "Where are you?"

"Look up."

So I do, glancing toward the building to my left, a squat green dormitory. My dorm building.

And there's Malik, standing on the fourth-floor common room balcony and staring down at me, his phone pressed to his ear.

"I was hoping someone would be cooking waffles up here, but no dice."

He's joking with me. That's good that he's joking, right? Could this mean . . .

"What are you really doing here?" I ask, my voice breath-less, my heart hammering hard—so dang hard—with hope. *Please* let him be here because he forgives me. *Please* let him give me another chance.

"Alex told me what dorm you were in," he said.

"You talked to Alex?"

"I went to her house. Her mother was kind enough to ring her on their house phone."

I just keep staring up at him, trying to make out his face, but this side of the building is in shadow.

"Meet me in the lobby," he says, disappearing into the build-ing and cutting off the call.

I nearly drop my bag so I can run faster, but I force myself to walk—a rushed walk, but at least it's not a sprint—into the lobby.

But it's empty. The elevators in our building are notoriously slow, and most of the time I take the stairs or I'll end up late for class. I contemplate running up the steps, taking them two at a time, all the way to the fourth floor where that balcony is. I can probably catch him still waiting for the elevator to arrive.

But instead, I force myself to stop next to a big saltwater tank, the bubbling of the air filter almost too quiet to be heard over my thundering heart. I stare at the waves of light the tank has created, counting backward from a hundred. I take deep breaths and smooth back my hair and straighten my hoodie.

Waiting.

At last, the elevator arrives with a *ding*, and he steps out.

He's so painfully beautiful, it steals my breath away.

He stops a few feet shy of me. I want to ask again why he's here, but instead I wait, staring into his eyes. Hoping that he's here to say he can't live without me, to ask me to be with him again, to say every day apart has been torture for him just like it has been for me.

"I figured it out," he says instead, shoving his hands into his pockets.

"Figured what out?"

"What I want to do. You know, how I'm going to give back. Make a difference."

I stare.

"That link you sent me, about the basket store?"

"Yeah?"

"Every basket they sell is handmade in an impoverished country. A *single store* in Seattle has created a demand for the product, and those people sell their baskets as fast as they can make them."

"I know, that's why I sent it to you. I thought maybe you could talk to the store owner or something. Maybe he would have some ideas for you."

"I did," Malik said. "And I realized what he's done has barely scratched the surface."

I narrow my eyes. "What do you mean?"

"It doesn't have to be just baskets. There are people all over the world with special skills. Wood carving. Weaving tapestries. Jewelry."

"But Buchannan Industries was founded on American-made," I say.

"I know. And I think our main Web site should stay that way. But I realized something."

"What?"

"I think the reason my grandfather was successful, even with his hand-written catalog, is that people want to help *people*, just like the mission statement says. Everyone is sick of buying plastic junk made in factories in China. They're tired of lining the pockets of rich CEOs while the blue-collar workers barely get by."

His eyes are blazing with such enthusiasm, such excitement, it's like he's come to life for the first time.

"We're going to create a subsidiary e-commerce site. One that features the stories and the skills of people all over the world. We'll sell their handmade wares at prices they could never command in their own region. We'll help them, but they're going to *help themselves*. It will be their work that gives them a better life. I'm just going to give buyers access to their products in a way that's not possible right now."

A smile tugs at my lips, and my chest tightens. "It's that whole teach-a-man-to-fish thing."

He grins, nodding. "All they need are customers. And I'm going to give them a worldwide storefront."

"That's . . . that's genius," I say. "It's everything you wanted."

"Because of you," he says, and the happiness simmers, darkens in his eyes as he steps closer to me. "See, here's the thing."

He falls silent, and I want to reach out, want to embrace him. But I'm afraid to move, afraid to fast forward and find out if his arrival here isn't actually the beginning of a make-up.

"When I figured this out, all I wanted was to tell you. To share it with you." He looks up at me, a tiny smile playing at the edges of his lips. "You were the one who believed in me. Who pushed me to figure it out. And so I got in my car and I drove six hours to see you."

He closes the distance between us until there's hardly a breath of air separating us, and I have to crane my neck to meet his gaze.

"Six hours is a long time. I did a lot of thinking," he says.

"And?"

"And today is National Positive Thinking Day."

I blink. "Is that a real thing?"

"Yes. We got lucky. I mean, I was hoping it was Grandiose Romantic Gesture Day, but no such luck."

Grandiose romantic gesture. Please let him be saying what I think he's saying.

"Okay . . . ," I say, trying to quell the urge just to kiss him. Trying to keep the hope from bubbling too high.

"And so, I was thinking we can make our relationship work. I mean, yeah, six hours is going to be a pain, but we could meet halfway sometimes, and there's always Skype. Besides, we have those plans to go to Disneyland over your next semester break."

I hurl myself against him, wrapping my arms around his body and pinning his own arms against him. And it's not until that moment that I realize how nervous he was, because it's almost like he melts against me in relief. The two of us nearly tumble to the ground before his legs scramble beneath him and we knock into the fish tank instead.

Luckily, it's too big to move.

"I love you," I whisper, my lips brushing against his neck.

I just breathe him in, that faint scent of cinnamon that I didn't even realize I'd been missing. It's not until a group of students tries to get past us that I let go.

"I love you too," he says as we pull apart. "You believed in me in a way no one ever has, and as soon as you were gone, it was like I didn't know what to do with myself. I'm sorry it took me this long to realize it . . . but I need you."

"I might forgive you," I say, unable to keep from grinning. "Is it really National Positive Thinking Day?"

"Yep. It's also Fortune Cookie Day, so I was kind of thinking we could go grab a bite to eat? It's not quite cooking-you-waffles-on-a-rooftop romantic, but . . ."

"It's perfect," I say, so happy I could burst. "Let's go."

As we step out into the sunshine, Malik's arm draped over my shoulders, I can't help but feel this is the beginning of my happily-ever-after.

ACKNOWLEDGMENTS

Although this may be my eleventh book, somehow it never gets easier. I owe many thanks to those who helped shepherd this story along.

My gratitude to: my agent, Bob Diforio, who brightens every day; my editorial team, Laura Whitaker and Sarah Shumway, without whom this book would be a mere shadow of itself; Jackson Pearce and Cyn Balog, who read an early draft and asked all the right questions; and last, but certainly not least, DeAndre Yedlin, who is so ridiculously good-looking he inspired the character of Malik.